IF ever in your life you are faced
with a choice, a difficult decision,
a quandary,

Ask yourself,
"What would Edgar and Ellen do?"

And do exactly the contrary.

Edgar & Ellen

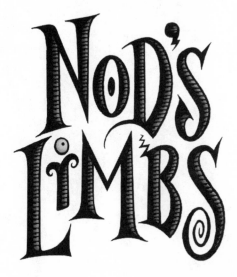

NOD'S LIMBS

Edgar & Ellen

NOD'S LIMBS

by
CHARLES OGDEN

illustrations by
RICK CARTON

ALADDIN
New York   London   Toronto   Sydney

Watch out for Edgar & Ellen in:

Rare Beasts
Tourist Trap
Under Town
Pet's Revenge
High Wire

❦ ALADDIN
An imprint of Simon & Schuster Children's Publishing Division
1230 Avenue of the Americas, New York, NY 10020
Copyright © 2006 by Star Farm Productions, LLC
All rights reserved, including the right of reproduction in whole or in part in any form.
Originally published in Great Britain in 2006 by Simon & Schuster UK Ltd, a CBS company.
ALADDIN and colophon are trademarks of Simon & Schuster, Inc.

Designed by Star Farm Productions, LLC.
The text of this book was set in Bembo, Auldroon, P22 Typewriter, Brighton, and Cheltenham.
The illustrations in this book were rendered in pen and ink and digitally enhanced in Photoshop.
Manufactured in the United States of America
First Aladdin edition February 2007
10 9 8 7 6 5 4 3 2 1
Library of Congress Cataloging-in-Publication Data
Ogden, Charles.
Nod's limbs / by Charles Ogden ; illustrated by Rick Carton.—1st Aladdin ed.
p. cm.—(Edgar & Ellen ; 6)
Summary: As they attempt to decipher a series of clues to buried treasure left by the founder of Nod's Limbs two hundred years before, twins Edgar and Ellen also race to find a cure for their pet, dying from the bite of Ellen's carnivorous plant.
ISBN-13: 978-1-4169-1501-0 (paper over board)
ISBN-10: 1-4169-1501-X (paper over board)
[1. Twins—Fiction. 2. Brother and sister—Fiction. 3. Buried treasure—Fiction. 4. Pets—Fiction. 5. Humorous stories.] I. Carton, Rick, ill.
II. Title. III. Series: Ogden, Charles. Edgar & Ellen ; 6.
PZ7.O333Nod 2007
[Fic]—dc22
2006006936

Here is my dedication—

I, Charles Ogden,
being of sound mind and body,
bequeath this book to my
personal inspirations for mischief:

To *Myron,* Imp the First,
I leave my last pack of poison,
and the unanswerable question
"For what is art, if not chaos?"

To *Uncle Johnny,*
I leave fish that can come out and play.

To *Cairo, Bain,* and *Van,* my Knights of the Brush,
I leave *Still Life with Moldy Cabbage and Eggs* and
the last gallon of Black Plague.

To *Jack, Liam,* and *Katy,*
I leave Granddad's wooden teeth and
the heirloom thimbles.

Finally, to everyone with and without
words of encouragement along the way,
I leave this sentimental reflection:
None of it could have been done without you.

—Charles

WHO KNOWS WHAT MIGHT APPEAR?

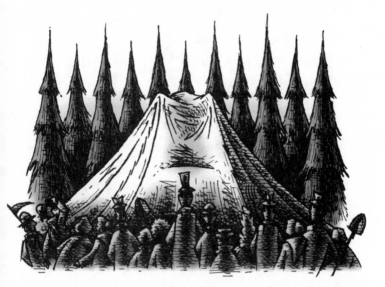

Nod's Lands

For the most part, Nod's Lands was a lovely place to live. It wasn't a big town, but it wasn't small either. It was, quite simply, an upstanding community of charming cottages and cheerful settlers, most of whom lived uneventful lives, making candles in the town's Waxworks.

Nestled as it was amid the lush Black Tree Forest and upon the banks of the Running River, Nod's Lands provided a comfortable, quiet place for its citizens to prosper. The days usually skipped along in a comforting sameness. But on this particular day, the town was atwitter. Augustus Nod, the odd, reclusive man who had founded the town many years earlier, had written a proclamation:

All citizens are advised that a most exquisite and splendorous sight shall be revealed henceforth in the park of our founder, this May 8, 1792, at 3 o'clock in the afternoon.

All who come will be enthralled.

The citizens rarely saw the father of their town. He lived on the outskirts in a tall, gray house topped by a cupola ringed with spikes. Not even the postman dared approach the mansion.

"Do you suppose he'll be here?" whispered the baker Opal Buffington. She and the rest of the townspeople waited patiently in Founder's Park before a twenty-foot-tall object covered by a tarp.

"Can't be sure, can we?" replied Millard Matterhorn, the managerial manager for the Waxworks. "He hardly shows his face at the 'Works anymore."

At the edge of the park, Nod's Lands' corpulent

mayor, Thaddeus Knightleigh, paced, huffing and grousing.

"I can't *believe* Nod held this ridiculous event without consulting me. I'm only *mayor of the town. I* should know what's under that tarp!"

"Quite, sir," said his footman, Robbins.

"*I* build the landmarks around here," said the mayor. "The clock tower, Town Hall . . . not *one* covered bridge, but *seven*! These stately public works fill the populace with awe! And whose idea was it to paint cheery messages on the bridges?"

"Yours," said Robbins.

"Of course! I give daily inspiration to my citizens. All Nod has given us is his name, and that is quite *enough*."

"Right as ever, sir."

Gonggg. Gonggg. Gonggg.

The crowd's murmurings ceased as the clock tower struck three. As the last gong faded into the warm afternoon, Thaddeus shifted his feet uneasily.

"Where is he?" the mayor whispered to himself.

A tall figure stepped from behind the tarped object. Faces fell when the townspeople saw that it was not the mysterious Augustus, but instead Mr. Hatfield Herringbottle, Esquire.

The gentleman cleared his throat.

"Good citizens of Nod's Lands! Our illustrious forefather was saddened that he could not join us today, but he has asked me, as his legal counsel, to host in his place the unveiling of a glorious monument for the eternal enjoyment of our town. Mr. Smithy, if you please."

Town builder Silas Smithy came forward, and, with a *whoosh,* removed the tarp.

The crowd gasped. There loomed a shining statue of Augustus Nod, seated on an imposing throne—and it appeared to be made of pure gold.

The dour-faced monolith seemed the exact likeness of the man they knew, down to the spider-shaped birthmark above his left eyebrow. But something else was unmistakably amiss. *He had no limbs.* No arms. No legs. No ringed fingers or buckled shoes.

"Silas! Where are the limbs?" demanded Hatfield Herringbottle.

"I know not, Mr. Herringbottle," said Silas Smithy, equally shocked. "Mr. Nod just had me cast the pieces—I didn't put the thing together. But as sure as you were born, I made arms and legs for that statue. A thief must have *stolen* the golden limbs!"

"Mr. Mayor," said Hatfield Herringbottle, "shall we form a search party?"

Thaddeus Knightleigh sized up the limbless statue and stifled a laugh. "Oh, I rather like it this way, don't you?"

But when he saw the concerned faces of his citizens, the mayor assumed a more serious expression. "Oh, very well. We shall fan out and search for these arms and legs ourselves. Perhaps they've only been misplaced." Thaddeus couldn't suppress a chuckle. "Hurry though! Before people start to call us Nod's *Limbs*."

1. Woe and Despair

"Nod's bods!" cried Edgar, throwing down his shovel. "We can't dig all this ourselves. We'll never reach the balm spring!"

His twin sister, Ellen, who had long since tossed her shovel aside, was clawing the dirt with her bare hands.

"We must . . . keep digging . . . or Pet . . . dies."

Edgar turned to look at the one-eyed hairball sitting on a nearby pile of rock. A hazy film coated its yellow eye, and its hair, though greasy and tangled as ever, now showed strands of gray. A poisonous bite from Ellen's carnivorous plant, Morella, and the subsequent destruction of the remaining balm (the mysterious, earthy goop Pet needed to survive) had left the creature hovering near death. The only cure lay in finding the source of the balm, which was beneath layers and layers of dirt.

"Sorry, Pet," said Edgar, plopping down beside the ailing creature. "This is all our fault."

Ellen glanced back at her brother. "We can't quit," she muttered. "We never quit."

But in the faint light of the lantern, Ellen could see the torn fingernails, scrapes, and blisters that told of their vain effort so far: Despite hours of digging, the twins had managed only a six-foot deep hole. Before the cave-in, the tunnel had dropped at least thirty feet.

"Bite your tongue, Sister." Edgar sighed. "No quitting. Just better planning."

"Planning?"

"Yes!" Edgar sat up a little. "Time to take advantage of our strategic strengths."

Ellen faced her brother and crossed her arms. "Shall we recap our *strategic strengths,* Brother? Hmm. Let's see. First, we plotted to collapse the Knightlorian Hotel and ended up securing its eternal purple existence."

"A minor setback."

"Then, we blew up Augustus Nod's laboratory and burned his journal to ashes."

"Words, words, words."

"And if memory serves," Ellen remarked, pointing to the mountain of dirt, "*I* caused this little cave-in."

"Now, Ellen, the ground was already unstable when you stomped your foot."

"And then when that crazy circus blew into town," Ellen continued, leaning into her sibling, "*you* got us suckered out of our own house!"

"It was a lousy sham," growled Edgar.

"Oh! Let's don't forget that we betrayed Heimertz and Dahlia and they've been imprisoned in a gorilla cage for life!"

The ever-smiling Ronan Heimertz, the former caretaker of the twins' house and grounds, had lived in a shed in the backyard. For years he had been the only person the twins feared, and they were relieved when his circus family had carted him and his girlfriend away on charges of attempted murder. Edgar and Ellen had discovered too late that Heimertz was innocent—the one person protecting both them and Pet.

At the mention of their loyal groundskeeper, Pet slipped off its perch and slunk dolefully toward the twins.

"We've spent years scheming against that vile Stephanie Knightleigh and her crooked family . . . and in the end, *they're* going to get the last laugh!"

Edgar stood up and took a deep breath. "So we regroup. We go back up to our house—"

"*Their* house, Edgar," Ellen interrupted. "The Knightleighs own it, remember? And by this time tomorrow, Eugenia Smithy and her crew will be swinging a wrecking ball at it. That's where our *strengths* have gotten us." Ellen plopped down on a pile of earth and scowled. Pet snuggled against her, and Ellen reached down to stroke its thinning hair. She winced as a few strands fell away but didn't say anything.

Edgar stared for a long moment at the rubble. Then he narrowed his eyes and cracked his knuckles.

"Don't say it, Brother. Don't you dare . . ."

"I have a plan, Sister."

"I knew you were going to say that."

2. Hugs and Kisses

"Operation: Jail Bail, ready for delivery."

Ellen sat at the large writing desk in the second-floor map room, placing a stamp on the letter she had just written.

"A rather clever scheme on such short notice," said Edgar. Out of pure habit, he tossed Pet in the air, then remembered too late the patient's delicate state. He caught the creature as gingerly as he could. "Heh, sorry there, Pet. But this two-pronged plan will give us time and muscle, the two things we need to unearth the balm spring and get you healthy."

Pet gamely waved a few hairs in encouragement, but then winced as if it had strained something.

Ellen read her letter aloud to Edgar:

> *Dear Heimertz (Ronan, that is—not any of you other Heimertzes who may be reading this),*
>
> *Sorry we got you in trouble with your family— especially the part when they chained you up and threw you in the cage. We thought you'd like to know that Edgar and I have a new home improvement project, and we are really digging into it with gusto. Also the Knightleighs are coming over soon for a big party, and I bet they're really going to bring the house down. Well, we hope your restraints aren't too tight. You sure know how to pick them, don't you?*
>
> *Hugs and kisses,*
> *Ellen*

"Hugs and kisses?" Edgar sneered. *"Blech."*

"It has to sound natural," said Ellen. "If someone is screening his mail, they can't suspect anything."

Pet nodded its eyeball.

"If you say so," said Edgar with a shrug, then gave one of the many map-room globes a spin. "So how do we send mail to a traveling circus?"

"They were heading west when they left town, right?" said Ellen. She consulted a tattered map on the wall marked NOD'S LANDS AND ENVIRONS, 1799. "Here's Nod's Limbs . . . and the next town west is . . . hmm."

On the outside of the envelope, she wrote:

To Ronan Heimertz
In custody of the Heimertz Family Circus
Greater Peaseblossom, or other points west
(Please forward. Don't make us come after you.)

As Ellen heated a glob of red wax to seal the enve-lope, Edgar produced a metal sliver no thicker than a pine needle from his satchel: a lock pick, his favor-ite escapist's tool. He placed it on the envelope, and Ellen dripped the wax onto it. She then stamped the wax with a seal, thus securing the little pick to the letter even while concealing it.

"Now for the second stage of our plan, Brother," said Ellen.

Edgar twirled a spark-plug wrench with his nimble fingers.

"To the Smithy & Sons Construction yard!"

"Let's hope it buys us time," said Ellen, and as the twins set out, they sang:

> *The seconds mock—tick, tock, tick, tock—*
> *So goes the heartless beating clock.*
> *Tick away till Knightleighs knock*
> *Our dwelling down to rubbled rock.*
> *Can Heimertz free us from this fate?*
> *Oh, if only time would wait!*
> *But never does the tock abate,*
> *Ticking toward Pet's deathly date.*
> *Somehow, some way we must defend*
> *Our home, our friend from dreary end.*

3. The Waxworks Beckons

After their visit to the Smithy & Sons construction yard, the twins took an alternate route home to throw potential snoops and sneaks off their tail.

Edgar grinned as he wiped olive paste off his footie pajamas.

"When Eugenia turns the key on her bulldozer tomorrow, she'll discover that olive paste does wonders for an ignition system," he said as they neared the old Waxworks. "Why can't every scheme go so smoothly, eh, Pet?" He gently lifted Pet out from his satchel, and placed it on his shoulder. The creature made a small noise, but Edgar couldn't tell if it was a snicker or a cough.

Ellen didn't reply; she had stopped in midstride and was pointing to the abandoned factory.

The grounds around the dilapidated building had, until recently, been host to the garish colors and boisterous sounds of the Heimertz Family Circus. But the carnival had left town after the big top's collapse, and neither Edgar nor Ellen had anticipated finding anything but darkness and quiet around the old factory.

Instead a fleet of unmarked white trucks clustered at the entrance to the Waxworks and a large crowd peered through the factory windows. Searing lights shone through the windows and the cracks in the walls.

"It can't be the circus, can it?" asked Edgar. "They

wouldn't return so soon after what happened."

"Even if they did," said Ellen, "that showboating Heimertz family would sooner travel on broken pogo sticks than in plain white trucks. Something else is going on."

"Less talking, more stalking," said Edgar, already slipping through the grass toward the building.

In its heyday the Waxworks had been a majestic building bustling with hardworking citizens making candles from dawn to dinnertime. But when Edgar and Ellen had previously explored the factory, they had seen no hint of its former glory. All that remained were decaying worktables; rusty candle-dipping contraptions; cobwebbed cogs and pulleys; and enormous vats of cooled, caked, crusty wax.

Edgar, Ellen, and Pet slipped past a handful of familiar locals: Executive Business Executive Marvin Matterhorn, Hotel Motel owners Mr. and Mrs. Elines, Buffy (proprietress of Buffy's Muffins), Sirs Malvolio and Geoffrey of the Renaissance reenacting Gallant Paintsmen, and several other of the siblings' former prank victims.

All of them jockeyed for position in front of the windows, eyes fixed on whatever was going on inside.

The twins ducked under a tape barrier marked DO NOT ENTER and sidestepped Nathan Ruby, rookie for the local yard maintenance squad, Lawn and Order, who was busy gulping down a chocolate muffin.

Another dodge or two brought the twins to a hiding spot behind an old, crusty vat.

"Brother, look!"

A handsome man with perfectly tousled hair raced across the factory floor on roller skates. He kept looking behind him at a pair of eight-foot-tall metal robots on wheels chasing him. Despite his too-thick makeup,

the man's features were immediately recognizable.

"Edgar," hissed Ellen. "It's, it's—"

"Blake Glide!"

4. Disquiet on the Set

Krshh-krshh-krshh-krshh.

Blake Glide skated as fast as his legs could go. The machines gained on him, their sharp pincers clacking with menace.

"Rarrrr!" hollered the robots through speakers on their heads. "Rarrr! Rarrr!"

"Submit now to . . . the Rollerbots!" called their leader.

"Never!" shouted Blake Glide. He *krshh*ed to the far side and reached the enormous, ten-foot vats marked WAX DIP. He backed against a vat as the Rollerbots drew closer.

"You've rolled your last, Earth Man!" burbled the lead monster through his tinny speaker.

Blake Glide turned a steely eye on his foes.

"That's what you think, you tanking tower of titan—er, titanic tank of—uh . . ."

"Cut!"

Famous film director Otto Ottoman threw his megaphone on the floor and stomped toward his star. Every member of his crew sighed and stepped away from their cameras and microphone booms.

"It's *towering tank of titanium!*" screamed the director. "How many times are we going to do this scene? Listen, B. G., the Rollerbots need to go to the bathroom, and that will take *two hours* in the costume department."

Edgar whispered to his sister, "I thought we'd scared that no-talent hack so badly he was never coming back here."

Blake Glide had once visited Nod's Limbs as part of the mayor's tourism initiative, but had left abruptly when he discovered the town was populated by man-eating aliens (or so the twins had led him to believe).

Blake Glide hung his head. "I'm sorry, Double O. I just can't concentrate. It's—"

"Don't tell me," snapped Otto Ottoman. "This town, this town, *this town!*" He jerked his head at the gaggle of spectators peeking through every factory window. "B. G., ever since you were cast in *Revenge of the Rollerbots*, you've been complaining about shooting in Ned's Limbs . . ."

"*Nod's* Limbs," corrected Blake Glide in a hushed

voice. He glanced fearfully at the legion of onlookers. "You don't know this place, Otto. But I do. And I should never have come back—"

"Look, it's not my fault your dinner theater investment went belly-up," said Otto Ottoman sternly. "Now *your* big-shot paycheck means *I* have to shoot on a budget smaller than *Attack of the Slurms*! You know, the studio wanted Dashiell Cragg from the beginning. I hear he's still available. . . ."

"Cragg?" said Blake Glide. "You *wouldn't*. He's no actor. . . . He's a chin dimple!"

"I *would*. They'll have my carcass if I waste any more time or money."

"But this place isn't right. Weird things happen here. Last time? They tried to . . . *eat me*."

"Blake, baby, I love your intensity. Keep that energy!" The director clapped his star on the back and sat down in his chair. "Someone oil Mr. Glide's skates!"

"No one ever believes me," muttered the star. But behind him two pajama-clad shadows stifled a snicker, and one of them whispered, "*We* believe you, old buddy."

"Did you hear that?" Blake Glide whipped his head around.

"Places, everyone!" the director bellowed, and everyone, even the reluctant star, complied.

For the first time the twins noticed that the cast and crew of *Rollerbots* were not the only occupants of the Waxworks. On the edge of the set, behind a barrier of velvet ropes and a sign reading VERY VIP SEATING, the twins spotted the beefy body of Mayor Knightleigh and his wife, Judith, flanked by their two children: Ellen's archnemesis, Stephanie, and her younger brother, Miles. As always, Stephanie wore a purple dress that complemented her perfect red curls; Miles, however, wore a foam hat shaped into a rough likeness of Blake Glide and clutched a pennant that read: NO. I GLIDEHEAD.

"Oh great. Princess Warts-for-Brains is here," said Ellen.

"Come on," said Edgar, crawling toward a golf cart marked FEATURE FILM DIRECTORS ONLY.

"What are you doing? We've got to get back to the caves," whispered Ellen.

"Oh, just one teensy prank? It's *Blake Glide*. What do you think, Pet?"

Pet nodded furiously, though it pained it to do so.

"Okay, okay, don't sprain your mustache," said

Ellen. "I suppose he does deserve a proper welcome. Here, use this brick for the accelerator."

Blake Glide skated back into position. A woman with a clapboard stepped in front of the camera and barked, "*Rollerbots*. Scene fifty-six. Take twelve."

She snapped the board with a crack, and Otto Ottoman cried, "Action!"

Blake Glide *krshh-krshh-krssh*ed across the floor again, wearing a convincing look of horror. The Rollerbots followed.

Edgar turned the ignition key on the golf cart and lined up the steering wheel.

"I christen thee the SS *Mayhem*," he said, patting the dashboard.

"Long may you sail," said Ellen, dropping the brick on the accelerator.

Thus did "one teensy prank" set off an extraordinary course of events that would change everything in Nod's Limbs forever.

5. Glide and Seek

The golf cart careened through the set, barreling across the director's chair, the assistant director's chair, the assistant assistant's chair, and finally, the Very VIP Seating. Cast and crew dove out of the way, and a thunderstruck Otto Ottoman buried his head in his hands.

"It's possessed by aliens!" screeched Blake Glide. "It'll kill us all!"

Stephanie pulled her brother onto a scaffold as their mother clambered to safety atop the soda machine. Their father dove for cover under a card table. Unfortunately his girth knocked out the legs of the flimsy table, and it collapsed, propped up by the mayor's belly.

The cart hit this homemade ramp and—with an agonized *"Oooof!"* from Mayor Knightleigh—flew through the air. It sailed across the room and landed just short of Blake Glide. The force of the landing tipped the floorboard like a seesaw and catapulted the terrified movie star across the factory.

"Talk about *sailing!*" said Ellen.

"Extra points for distance," said Edgar.

Even Pet managed an excited hop on Edgar's shoulder.

Screaming like a howler monkey, Blake Glide crashed through a door marked A. NOD, PROPRIETOR.

"My star!" cried Otto Ottoman.

"My hero!" cried Miles Knightleigh.

"My stomach!" cried Mayor Knightleigh.

Miles was the first through the broken door, followed by a camera crew and one dismayed director. The pack of curious Nod's Limbsians who had been huddled outside the windows now pushed inside to see the calamity for themselves. The movie star had flown headfirst through an oil painting on the opposing wall. It was a portrait of Augustus Nod, and Blake Glide's thrashing legs protruded from Nod's mouth like a forked tongue.

"Quick," called Otto Ottoman. "Call Dashiell Cragg!"

Miles grabbed his idol by the skates and pulled. "Talk to me, Mr. Glide! Don't go toward the light!"

"Gormph!" responded Blake Glide. Several townspeople joined Miles in dragging the movie star from the hole. He fell to the ground, moaning through a mouthful of canvas.

Mayor Knightleigh hastened into the crowded office. "What kind of two-bit Tinseltown operation are you trying to pawn off on us, Ottoman? I should

have you run in for attempted mayorcide!"

The twins peered in from the doorway.

"Nothing like the wail of an action hero to brighten up the day," said Edgar. Pet bristled in agreement.

"Don't you mean 'flail'?" asked Ellen, grinning.

"How about 'jail'?" yelled Stephanie Knightleigh behind them. "I just *knew* I'd find you menaces lurking around here. And now you're *busted* for the last time—"

"GOLD!" cried Blake Glide.

Silence fell as the action star hobbled to his feet and reached through the ripped painting. He pulled out a small ingot of sculpted gold. The crowd gasped audibly, for every Nod's Limbsian recognized what it was: a tiny replica of the limbless statue of Nod that sat in Founder's Park. This figurine, however, was decidedly *limbed*.

"Wonder of wonders," said Buffy. "So *that's* what it was supposed to look like."

"What else is in there?" asked Marvin Matterhorn. "More gold?"

Blake Glide was already rooting around inside the wall, but Miles examined the painting's ornate frame.

"Hey, it swings out," he said. "It's a secret vault, just like the ones at our house, Dad!"

Mayor Knightleigh chuckled nervously, but no one seemed to notice. Instead Otto Ottoman pushed his star away from the hole long enough to swing the painting out. Just as Miles had said, a large compartment lay within, like a hidden safe. The lighting crew turned the spotlights on its contents: a porcelain ink pot, a spiny quill, a wax mold, wax copies of the statue, and a pile of yellowed papers.

The paper on top of the stack bore an elaborate

stamp made from gold leaf that read: WILL AND TES-
TAMENT. The onlookers gasped.

Blake Glide, Mayor Knightleigh, Otto Ottoman,
and a few others reached for the papers all at once.
But before their fingers could touch anything, a
ringing voice froze them in place.

"Do not touch that document!" cried a frail old
man. He prodded through the crowd with a silver-
tipped walking cane until at last he stood before the
vault. He buttoned his suit jacket and straightened
his crisp necktie.

"Be this Augustus Nod's, or be it not," began the
man, "a final testament of any kind is a sacred thing.
This is a matter for the law, and none other."

"I played Louie 'the Law' Lindman in *Legal
Weapon*," boasted Blake Glide, his hand extended.
"So I'm sure I'm qualified to—"

"Hands to yourself, Mr. Glide!" warned the
old man. "So says the senior partner of the law
firm Herringbottle, Pratt, and Filbert. I am Lyman
Herringbottle, and my great-great-great-great-great-
great-great-grandfather wrote this will at the behest
of Augustus Nod himself. Should this sheaf of paper
prove authentic, it may very well be the single most
important document in Nod's Limbs' history."

6. The Reading of the Will

"Mr. Herringbottle, I assure you," said Mayor Knightleigh, "this couldn't possibly be the *real* will of Augustus Nod. Everybody knows he went insane and disappeared. He never left a will."

"Not that anyone found," Lyman Herringbottle corrected. He lifted the paper gingerly, and his eyes sparkled. "Herringbottle family legend has long told of the lost will and what would happen if it were ever recovered."

"What . . . what *would* happen?" asked the mayor. His face had gone pale.

"That, good sir . . . ," began Lyman Herringbottle. He removed his red handkerchief from his breast pocket and dusted off the imposing wooden chair behind the desk, then hiked his pant legs and sat down. ". . . is a singular tale, indeed."

The old man withdrew an unlit pipe from his jacket and clenched it in his teeth. He carefully examined the yellow paper. "Yes, yes, the seals are genuine!"

Several people in the crowd gasped.

"My ancestor, Hatfield Herringbottle, was Nod's Limbs' first lawyer, and one of Augustus Nod's few confidants," Lyman Herringbottle said grandly. "Oh, the tales whispered down from generation to generation in the Herringbottle households! They tell of a Nod descending into madness, a Nod who wrote the most curious of last wishes, a Nod with a . . . *golden* secret."

"More gold?" asked Blake Glide, and everyone in the room seemed to tense.

"Sadly," said the lawyer, "Nod disappeared before entrusting his final testament to the hands of his lawyer. For all Hatfield knew, Nod had taken the will with him wherever he had gone. To find it after all this time . . . Well, we are all witness to history this day. I ask you: Shall I now give this document the public reading it has been deprived of for two hundred years?"

"No need for that—" began Mayor Knightleigh, but he was drowned out by a loud "YES" from the crowd. The townspeople and movie crew pressed closer as the lawyer carefully untied the string that bound the papers.

With great care and deliberation, Lyman Herringbottle placed a pair of reading glasses on the bridge of his nose and squinted. He licked his lips and pursed them several times before he began to read.

"October 13, 1802," he began. "My dearest idiots—"

"Now really!" cried Mayor Knightleigh. "Must we hear the ravings of this kook? He squandered his fortune on crazy schemes, and went as bonkers as a bedbug by the end! What's the point of entertaining this further?"

The movie crew, and even a few Nod's Limbsians, turned and gave the mayor the most gusty "shh!" he had ever received. He deflated as Herringbottle cleared his throat and continued.

> *My dearest idiots of Nod's Lands, or Limbs, or any which whatever you are,*
>
> *I am dead and you are not. Well done! Whatever will you do for an encore?*
>
> *If things have gone according to plan, you are now gathered in the sylvan glade of Founder's Park, and my legal counsel, the estimable Hatfield Herringbottle, is reading this aloud to all who care to hear it. Speak up, Herringbottle, they cannot hear you in back!*

"Yes! Speak up, Herringbottle!" shouted Marvin Matterhorn. "We can't hear you in back!"

"Oh, yes, excuse me," said Lyman Herringbottle, reading on slightly louder.

> *A will is often an old man's chance to divide up his possessions among his loved ones, choosing who will get, say, Granddad's wooden teeth and who the heirloom thimbles. Of course, I have no loved ones, surrounded as I am by such dolts and cattleprods as the people of this hapless hamlet. Sheep, the lot of you! Not a unique thought in any of your pumpkin heads! Following blindly that blackguard mayor of yours—*

"Uh, does he say who gets the little statue?" Blake Glide interrupted. "Because if he doesn't mention it, I *am* the finder. . . ."

Lyman Herringbottle harrumphed as he scanned the pages. "He does seem to go on at length about his fellow citizens. . . . Oh my! Shameful language! . . . I don't even know what that . . . Ah, here, it picks up a bit on page four."

*Perhaps I have been wrong, and there is one
with the intellect and backbone I seek. But he
(or she) will have to prove himself (or herself).
Can I discover this from beyond the mortal
coil? Yes. Bless me, I can.*

I propose a contest. Find the golden limbs.

*Oh, I know well where they lie, for it was
I who took them. I! Why should a whole
and complete statue of Nod be bequeathed
to the very town that took so much from the
living Nod, leaving him incomplete, less than
himself? Thus I reasoned, and the night before
the limbs were to be joined to my statue, I
hid them. Knowledge of their location shall
die with me; I have left only six little verses,
and they are rigidly tight-lipped on the matter.
These verses—one of which you shall find
in this very document—are riddles, clues, and
mental puzzlings to vex and confound you,
yes, but also to guide you.*

*Whosoever finds these limbs has earned my
approval, dead though I may be. The statue*

belongs to the town as ever, but, Successful
Hunter, the limbs are yours, as are each and
every one of my possessions, from gold coin to
coniferous fir.

If you citizens of Nod's Limbs are as dense
and dim as I suspect, you will earn all you
deserve—naught but misery! I'll wager my
weight in candlewax that greed and betrayal
will tear you apart before you find a thing!
Still, perhaps . . . perhaps . . . one of you is
clever enough to carry on in my name. Good
fortune. Or no fortune.

Yours nevermore,
Augustus Nod

"My, oh my," whispered Buffy.

"Mine, all mine," murmured Otto Ottoman.

"So that includes the little statue?" asked Blake
Glide.

7. The First Clue

Murmurs spread through the crowd.

"What a waste of time," called Mayor Knightleigh over the buzz. "Everyone knows the old scoundrel squandered his fortunes and died penniless—there were no 'gold coins or coniferous firs' left! What point would there be in winning his possessions now?"

"Well, that's not true," whispered Edgar to his sister. "There are lots of firs on our property, and we know Nod owned that."

"Shh, Brother," said Ellen. "Apparently *they* don't know that!"

"Daddy, you're forgetting the limbs!" said Stephanie. "Whoever finds them, keeps them!"

The mayor peered disapprovingly at his daughter, but others were already nodding in agreement.

"Those limbs would be quite valuable," said Marvin Matterhorn. "Think of the businesses that could be launched and mercilessly franchised!"

"Or the number of shiny, candy-apple tractor mowers we can add to our fleet!" said Lawn and Order's Chief Strongbowe.

"Gramercy!" exclaimed Sir Malvolio. "Golden victory shall restore the Gallant Paintsmen to former glory! To the riddle, man! Hence!"

"Right you are, right you are," said Lyman Herringbottle, turning the pages of the will.

"Well?" cried Otto Ottoman. "Don't keep it to yourself. Read it out loud!"

"Yes, yes, I was getting to that," said Lyman Herringbottle. "No need to be rude. See here—he's written it out on this last page. It reads:

> The stolen limbs you hope to find—
> The secret, then: to read my mind.
> My golden effigy holds the key
> That will begin the mystery.
> So peer thee inward, where I think
> You will find the missing link.

The room was quiet for a moment until Blake Glide moaned and threw his arms in the air.

"Oh, it's hopeless! Impossible to solve. The gold is lost forever!"

"What's an 'f and g,' Stephie?" asked Miles, pulling on his sister's sleeve.

"Not 'f and g,' Miles," said Stephanie. "'Effigy.' It's another word for something that looks like someone, like a doll . . . or a statue."

"A *golden* statue," said Nathan Ruby.

"By Jupiter, he's right!" exclaimed Marvin Matterhorn. "Nod's golden statue in Founder's Park. Ingenious!"

"Now that's just fun," said Fire Chief Gully Lugwood. "A treasure hunt is going to be a big hit with my kids, I can tell you."

"It'll be a hit with the whole town!" said Buffy. "Why, I'll bet we'll all have a hoot of a time solving this thing *together*."

Several of his fellow citizens nodded in agreement, though the film crew, the Knightleighs, and the twins expressed varying degrees of disgust.

"Hey, where's B. G.?" asked Otto Ottoman. His eyes darted in every direction, but Blake Glide had vanished. Just then, tires squealed outside as a car pulled away in a hurry.

"Scoundrel!" said Sir Malvolio. "He's on the hunt!"

8. Lost and Founder

The cluster of cars outside the Waxworks dispersed like the sparks off a firework.

"Let's make this an orderly procession!" called Police Chief Gomez. "Keep your peepers open for those pedestrians!"

"Let me through!" yelled Mayor Knightleigh out the window of his limousine. "The mayor goes to the front of any line!"

A stream of cars rolled onto the street, including a van full of Rollerbot parts and buckets of makeup. The driver and his front-seat passenger, two of the movie crew, were arguing about hidden meanings in the riddle, and didn't hear the murmurs of two stowaways in back.

"Looks like we're the only ones who know Nod didn't die *totally* penniless, despite what Knightleigh thinks," said Ellen.

"Sister, if we find the limbs, we get everything, including his house. *Our* house," said Edgar. "Knightleigh may own the deed—but it'll be worthless!"

"And with the gold, we'll have enough money to buy a steam shovel. We'll save Pet *and* our house in one fell swoop!" Ellen pulled Pet from the satchel and held aloft the little lump. "Rest easy, Pet. There's just a simple battle of brains between us and these treasure hunters."

Pet tapped Ellen's forehead with a lock of hair.

"A war of wits," said Edgar, "and everyone else is unarmed."

The van pulled up to a stop. The twins tucked Pet into Edgar's satchel and ducked out the back. On the trim green lawn of Founder's Park, the imposing statue of limbless Nod gazed down with reproach at the people hurrying toward him.

Blake Glide stood by the statue, hands in his pockets and whistling with unconvincing innocence. The bronze nameplate in the base, which read NOD: FOUNDER OF NOD'S LIMBS, 1742—? had been wrenched off the front and thrown on the grass.

"What's happened to our statue?" cried Chief Strongbowe.

"It was like that when I got here, I swear," said Blake Glide.

"Public property defaced!" cried Mayor Knightleigh as he hustled onto the grounds. "This treasure hunt has gone from farce to civic nuisance."

Marvin Matterhorn ran to the statue and examined the space where the nameplate had been.

"There's a little compartment here! Just like the nook behind the oil painting," he said. "But I don't feel anything inside. It's empty."

"Of course it is," said the mayor. "I'm telling you this whole business is a hoax! There's no clue in this statue!"

Disappointed murmurs rippled from the crowd.

"I suppose you're right, Mr. Mayor," said Fire Chief Gully Lugwood. "We shouldn't have gotten our hopes up to find some old clue—"

"Unless *he* has it," said Otto Ottoman, pointing at Glide. "You were here first, B. G. You didn't pocket the clue on these good folks now, did you?"

Blake Glide's jaw dropped and he clutched his chest. "Double O! I'm shocked! You don't really think—"

The Nod's Limbsians were just as appalled.

"That . . . that wouldn't be fair!"

"Movie stars would never be dishonest. Would they?"

"If we can't trust a famous person, who *can* we trust?"

But the members of the film crew—seemingly not

ready to trust a movie star—set upon Blake Glide.

"I didn't steal anything!" he protested, as the crew turned out his pockets. Expensive moisturizers, an empty money clip, and a variety of breath mints fell to the ground—but no gold.

During the distraction, Edgar and Ellen tiptoed up to the statue's base and gazed into the dark recess.

"They didn't examine the statue very closely," said Ellen. "Sloppy work."

"Typical townies. No doubt they missed something," said Edgar, fishing a flashlight from his satchel. "Let's shed a little light on things."

The light revealed a small compartment chiseled into the granite base, the perfect place to store a clue. Aside from dust, however, the nook was bare. Edgar and Ellen exchanged puzzled glances.

At last, the search of Blake Glide's pockets, wallet, and socks came up empty for stashed clues.

The mayor waved his arms. "Upstanding citizens, can't you see the chaos this treasure hunt is already causing in our town? First there's the, er, disfigurement of this fine statue. And the way many of you drove over here . . . well, twenty-five miles per hour *indeed*. Now unwarranted pocket searches? We can't afford further disquiet. By the authority vested in me

by the mayor—who is me—I am officially shutting down this nonsense."

But none of the upstanding citizens seemed to hear. They milled about the statue, mumbling to themselves and rubbing their chins in thought.

Stephanie Knightleigh walked behind the twins and hissed in their ears. "Enjoy your last night in your snug little beds," she said. "If I had my way, you'd be chained to them when the wrecking ball hits tomorrow."

Edgar reached into the satchel and pulled out a pipe wrench. He smacked it in the palm of his hand. Stephanie sneered.

"You don't have the guts," she said, turning her back on the twins. She walked back toward the family limo.

"Brother, what were you planning to do with that?" asked Ellen. "A wrench attack would have been so . . . *Knightleigh* of you."

"This isn't for her," said Edgar. "I have an idea. We just need this crowd to clear out."

"ATTENNNNNTION-TION-TION!" The announcement echoed so loudly that the treasure hunters stopped talking and covered their ears. Red-faced Mayor Knightleigh stood by his limousine with a bullhorn in his hands. The volume, it seemed, had been turned all the way up. "THE HUNT IS OVER-ER-ER. THERE IS NOTHING-ING-ING TO SEE HERE-ERE-ERE. THERE IS NO!-O!-O! GOLD!-OLD!-OLD! NOW SKEDADDLE-ADDLE-ADDLE!"

9. Gold-Brained

The would-be hunters shuffled away from the statue. The mayor, returning to normal color, patted the disappointed citizens on their backs as they went.

"Now, now," he said. "What on earth would anyone do with a golden limb anyway? And goodness, it's almost eight thirty. Bedtime! Tomorrow this will all seem so silly."

The Nod's Limbsians filed out of the park, followed by the film crew. ("Man, the things these small town yokels do for fun.") The twins returned to the foot of the statue.

"Now we strike," whispered Edgar. "Remember what the riddle said about the statue?"

"Sure," said Ellen. "The riddle is inside. And

none of these simpletons looked for a secret compartment in the statue itself—*Watch out!*" Ellen pulled her brother behind a bush as Chief Strongbowe shone his flashlight through the park to ensure the last of the stragglers was headed home.

"Yes, a secret compartment—but not just anywhere," said Edgar. "Remember the exact words: 'So peer thee inward, where I think/You will find the missing link.' *Peer where I think*, Sister!"

Ellen nodded. "'The secret then; to read my mind.' It's in his head!"

Edgar and Ellen scaled the statue and examined the figure's head, using Edgar's flashlight. Edgar gently tapped the chin, the nose, and the ears with his pipe wrench.

"A very delicate process, Sister. Only a well-trained ear can pick out details like the thickness of the metal . . . the flaws in the structure . . . the hollow spots within—*Hey!*"

Ellen yanked the wrench away.

"No mystery, Edgar. It's in his head!" she said, and she gave the golden forehead a mighty whack.

Gong!

The golden head rang like a church bell. The twins slapped their hands over their ears.

As the echoes waned to a dull hum, the twins heard a soft clattering sound. Nod's eyes had fallen back inside his head, and now the statue stared out with eerie, empty sockets.

Edgar shone the light into the right eye and peered in. "We were right! A riddle, carved into the back of his head! We've done it, Sister!"

"Read it to me," said Ellen, seizing charcoal and paper from the satchel. "Quick!"

Edgar moved the light to and fro and began to read:

> *Always telling, never talking.*
> *Always running, never walking.*
> *But on her limbs she bears a clue*
> *She will not yield to show to you.*

"Okay, did you get that?" he asked.

"Got it!" said a voice from below. The twins looked down to see a woman writing in a spiral notebook. She stood next to a man with a camera around his neck. "Fancy sleuthing, you two! Can't wait for our readers to get a load of this!"

Before the twins could react, a flash blinded them, just long enough for Nancy Weedle, star reporter of the *Nod's Limbs Gazette*, and photographer Snap Watson to hurry out of the park, taking the story of the century with them.

10. Demolition Day

The twins slumped on their beds while an exhausted Pet dozed in the satchel.

"Come sunrise, the whole town will get the second riddle in their morning paper," said Ellen. "We need to solve it *now*."

"It's obvious, right? 'Always running, never walking.' It's the Running River."

"Of course. But where, Brother? It's nothing but a long, muddy stream. The riddle mentions limbs. Are they the other little creeks that flow into this one?"

"Perhaps, or the banks of the beach. What is that 'Always telling, never talking' business?"

"A reference to a babbling brook? Maybe the Running River wasn't always such a quiet trickle."

"If so, Nod might have tied the clue around a brick and sunk it into the riverbed."

The twins debated methods of dredging the river until their eyelids grew heavy and they fell asleep.

In the early hours of dawn, a low rumble echoed through their house. It was the sound of approaching machinery.

Edgar opened one eye. "No. *No!*"

Ellen leaped to the window. "Bulldozers! Dump trucks! A *wrecking ball*! Why didn't the olive paste work?"

Down below, a woman in coveralls and a hard hat strode up to the house and plunked a metal pail onto the front steps. An oily green slop sloshed onto the ground.

"Hey, twins! You misplaced your snack!"

"Blasted Eugenia Smithy!" Ellen snarled. "Impossible to fool."

"Edgar! Ellen! Out of the house!" Eugenia called. "Today is doomsday for your domicile!"

"Failure most bitter!" cried Edgar.

But his sister was already halfway down the stairs. Edgar hurried after her.

"What are you going to do?" he asked.

"Our best weapon now," Ellen said, "is greed."

The twins stepped out to meet the construction forewoman face-to-face. Instead of sneering or scowling or baring her nails, as she was often wont to do, Ellen looked calm.

"I'm surprised you're at work today, Eugenia," said Ellen.

"I doubt you're surprised by much, Ellen," said Eugenia. Several other construction workers approached cautiously. Eugenia spoke to them over her shoulder. "These are the ones. Be careful, like I told you. They won't go quietly."

"Oh, of course we will," said Ellen. "We don't have time to dawdle around here. We've got to find the *gold* before the rest of the town does."

"Gold?" asked one of the workers.

"You didn't hear about the treasure hunt? It was in all the papers. Nod's will has been found, and it's riddled with riddles. They point the way to the missing *solid gold* limbs of Nod's statue. Whoever finds them gets to keep them."

The workers eyed one another to see if anyone was buying the story.

"Nice bluff," said Eugenia. "I expected an attack of poison arrow frogs, or Hungarian biting flies maybe. But a distraction tactic, that's new—"

"'Always telling, never talking,'" began Edgar. "'Always running, never walking.'"

"'But on her limbs she bears a clue she will not yield to show to you,'" Ellen finished.

"What was that?" asked a bushy-mustached worker.

"The next riddle in the hunt," said Ellen. "I wish we could figure it out, but it's just so hard."

The man stroked his mustache. "Well, see . . . 'always running, never walking.' That . . . that's the Running River, I reckon."

Eugenia glowered. "Doggone it, Steve—"

"Okay, but what about the rest of it?" asked a thick-necked man. "What kind of limbs does a river have?"

"I guess that just means the banks," said Steve. "Hey, what about the beach? That's where *I'd* bury treasure if I had some to bury."

Edgar, Ellen, and the other workers all agreed that was a brilliant idea, and congratulated Steve for his quick thinking. Despite Eugenia's protests, the group took a quick vote and determined that the house demolition could wait another few hours while they searched the beach. Edgar produced an old shovel and presented it to the team.

"This should make quick work of all that sand," he said. The men grabbed it and made for the river, whooping.

The twins followed, leaving Eugenia Smithy alone on the front stoop. As they ran they sang:

The search is on! The treasures call
Somewhere beneath the sandy sprawl.
So do put down that wrecking ball—
You've got a beach to comb!
The shrewdest only shall behold
Scads of riches, wealth untold.
(Plus if you're on the hunt for gold,
You can't tear down our home!)

11. Down by the River

When Edgar and Ellen arrived at the Running River, however, their high spirits plummeted.

It seemed every citizen of Nod's Limbs had read the riddle in the morning paper and had come to the same conclusion. Treasure hunters clogged the beach, and many others paced the riverbank on both sides. The high school football team examined the north bank by crawling along in a sort of practice-drill exercise while the residents of the Nod's Limbs Retirement Community scoured the beach with metal detectors. Blake Glide and the movie crew could be seen burrowing with film canisters as Sirs Malvolio and Geoffrey used paint trays to scoop sand

and pan it for gold. Children with plastic shovels and buckets scampered everywhere, picking up random scraps of trash and taking them to Janitor Clunch, who held a sign that read: IF IT ISN'T A CLUE, IT'S LITTER.

"What a way to spend a Saturday!" said Betty LaFete.

"Such an educational game!" gushed school-teacher Suzette Croquet. "Riddles to tickle my little students' minds!"

"I'm gonna find that gold, you betcha!" said little Timmy Poshi. Miss Croquet smiled and patted him on the head.

Ellen groaned. "What sickening displays of civic teamwork."

"Sister, we have to clear this place out so we can search in private," said Edgar. "If only I had some Hungarian biting flies . . ."

"No time," said Ellen. "Start digging, before one of these simpletons finds our golden ticket!"

The twins plunged their own shovels into the sand, just like the others around them.

As the horde of hunters grew, Principal Mulberry of Nod's Limbs Grammar School climbed a stepladder and spoke through a megaphone. The townspeople politely stopped their digging to listen.

"Greetings, fellow treasure hunters!" she cried to hails of cheering. "I'm really happy with the town-wide participation we're seeing. Now to keep the proceedings from getting disorderly, how about we add a dose of our classic Nod's Limbs *cooperation!*"

More cheers from the masses. The twins redoubled their shoveling while everyone else was preoccupied.

Principal Mulberry cleared her throat. "That's super, everyone! Well, the PTA and I thought that the best way to give everyone a chance to play this game was to divide ourselves into teams!" She smiled and nodded at the rousing applause. "Let's crack this nut together!"

With Principal Mulberry presiding over the process, several groups took shape. The football team and the marching band joined together to become Team Gridiron. A cluster of women from the retirement center became the Silver Lining Ladies, and the Cairo Avenue shopkeepers dubbed themselves the Bottom-Dollar League. The Teacher-Janitor Alliance pledged a tight union ("Wise minds! Clean schools! Golden future!"), while Sir Malvolio and Chief Strongbowe merged the Gallant Paintsmen and Lawn and Order to forge the Gauntlet.

Groups of school-age children were divided evenly into teams. Miles Knightleigh had donned the pirate hat he won at the Heimertz Family Circus, and suggested his group be called the No-Quarter Pirates. His teammates endorsed the idea, and with cries of "Yarr!" and "Yo ho, ho!" they brandished sticks in the air like cutlasses. (Upon further reflection, however, they decided "no quarter," which means "no mercy," might give other hunters the wrong impression, so they opted for the much more considerate *Some*-Quarter Pirates.)

At last Principal Mulberry made the teams official

by recording them all on her clipboard. Then the hunt began anew—after a countdown and a whistle to "give things a proper beginning."

Meanwhile the twins had stopped their aimless digging to observe the spectacle.

Ellen leaned on her shovel and pulled a pigtail. "We're missing something," she said at last. "Everyone in this town came to the river because the clue seemed so easy. But it would be just like Nod to lead people astray."

"Good point, Sister," said Edgar. "If these dim-wits think this is the place, then it *can't* be right."

So as Mayor Knightleigh pulled up in his limo ("Great buttered biscuits! Can't a mayor sleep in on a Saturday without his town going berserk?"), the twins retreated from the cheery bustle to review the riddle.

"'Always running, never walking,'" said Ellen. "What else runs all the time?"

"Your mouth," said Edgar.

"'Always telling, never *talking*,'" said Ellen, smooshing her brother's face into the dirt.

Edgar laughed and wiped his face. "Okay, okay. What's always running? Refrigerators. Respirators. Hotels. Clocks. Sewage treatment plants."

"Great, but none of those things can speak," mused Ellen.

"*Telling* and *talking* aren't necessarily the same thing," said Edgar. "When you sneak up behind me, I can *tell* you're there from the stench."

"Can you *tell* what I'm going to do next?" Ellen balled up her fist for another sisterly pummel, but froze midstrike. Her wide eyes grew even wider.

Edgar peeked out from behind his arms.

"Brother," said Ellen. "I have the answer."

"Well, it's about time, Sister!"

Ellen smirked. "Exactly."

12. The Wisdom of the Pirates

Mayor Knightleigh realized his attempts to shoo everyone back to their homes were futile. The formation of the teams had brought organization and energy to the search as teammates cheered one another on, conferred on best locations to dig, and took shifts to stay fresh. The hunt was now an unstoppable force, and the mayor could do nothing but fume in the back of his limo.

"Disorder, disorder, disorder!" he raved.

Before long the entire length of each riverbank was pockmarked with holes, but no second clue had been found. Treasure hunters leaned on their shovels in exhaustion.

"I have scoop blisters," whined Timmy Poshi.

"I have sand between my perfectly straight teeth!" wailed Blake Glide. *"Where is that clue?"*

That's when the Some-Quarter Pirates trooped up to Principal Mulberry and asked to use her megaphone.

"Um, yo ho ho, everyone," said Calvin Hucklebee in a meek voice. "The Some-Quarter Pirates, we, uh . . . uh, we had, well, an idea."

"Don't be shy, little fella!" said Chief Strongbowe. "Pipe right up!"

"Well, we looked at the clue again, and it seemed to some of us that, well, there are other kinds of things that run," said Calvin Hucklebee. "First, Donald Bogginer said that the air conditioner in his house is always running, which made Burl Turkle think of how his watch always runs too. And then I was like, 'Hey, can you tell time on that, 'cause, like, I only use digital—'"

"What's your point?" shouted Blake Glide.

Miles Knightleigh leaned into the megaphone.

"Avast, mateys, the next clue be at the clock tower!"

"Miles!" roared Mayor Knightleigh as he wriggled out of his limo. But the crowd's noise drowned him out.

"Hey!" cried Nathan Ruby. "The tykes are right! Clocks are always *running,* and they always *tell* time."

"Well met, small rogues!" cheered Sir Malvolio.

"Nifty!" shouted Sir Geoffrey.

"The clock tower was around in Nod's day," Janitor Clunch concluded. "That must be the answer!"

Chief Strongbowe pointed down Florence Boulevard.

"To the clock tower! And don't trample the petunia beds!"

13. Tooth by Tooth

The Some-Quarter Pirates were escorted to a place of honor at the front of the throng, and the children led the parade, swinging and swashing their pretend cutlasses. Blake Glide, Otto Ottoman, and the movie crew joined in, though they looked rather annoyed, and a grumbling mayor brought up the rear. On the way, the hunters chatted about how obvious the riddle now seemed.

"'But on her limbs she bears a clue she will not yield to show to you,'" recited Marvin Matterhorn. "That's a reference to the clock's hands, you see? The next clue must be written on them. Elementary, really."

The Nod's Limbs clock tower—commissioned by Mayor Thaddeus Knightleigh himself—had stood at the edge of town for more than 200 years. As the crowd approached, its heavy black hands were swinging upward toward the noon hour.

The pirates threw open the door at the foot of the tower and led the parade up a narrow, spiraling staircase. Above them, sunlight streamed through the translucent clock face, onto the guts of the clockworks, alternately casting them in warm light and cold shadows.

A girl in striped footie pajamas appeared on the staircase ahead of them, blocking the way.

"Sorry, folks, nothing to see here," she said. "The clock tower is being fumigated for an infestation of cuckoo wasps. You better clear out before clouds of noxious gas cause a sudden outbreak of death."

Many in the crowd groaned in disappointment.

"What rotten timing," said Chief Strongbowe. "Well, folks, safety first."

"Are you crazy?" cried Blake Glide from several flights down. "Why would you believe the weird girl in the pajamas?"

"Now, now," said Principal Mulberry. "Here in Nod's Limbs we don't judge others by their sleep-wear."

"Look!" yelled Otto Ottoman. "There's another one!"

Indeed a boy in matching striped pajamas could be seen in the clockworks, clinging to the tooth of a gear that was rotating slowly upward. The townspeople weren't sure what he was up to, but it certainly looked nothing like fumigation. The moviemakers in the mob surged forward, propelling the Nod's Limbsians with them. Ellen found herself shoved aside as the treasure hunters rushed to a land-ing near the top of the clock's face.

If the face had been transparent, the hunters would have had an excellent view of Nod's Limbs from their lofty perch. But the only thing visible through the giant opaque plate was the shadow of the clock's hands, which were drawing very near to twelve o'clock.

The cog from which Edgar now dangled was propelling the minute hand—and Edgar—closer to the numeral "12." Blake Glide elbowed his way to the fore, and leaned over the rail.

"What is that little gremlin doing?" Blake Glide asked.

The cogs continued their slow turn. A half-minute more and Edgar's hands would be crushed between the teeth of the gears. He risked a glance at the clock face behind him.

There, just below the twelve, a small window no bigger than a thumb was cut into the face. When the clock struck twelve, the window would reveal the back of the hour hand. Edgar was perfectly placed to see it—

"Yow!" hollered Edgar, as Stephanie landed on his fingers. She had lashed one sleeve of her lavender sweater to a cog-driving shaft above Edgar and swung across to the gear. "Get off!"

"Oh, excuse me," said Stephanie, digging her heel into Edgar's knuckles.

Tock. Tock. Tock.

The gear continued to climb, the tocks echoing through the tower. Edgar bit his tongue, ignoring the pain in his fingers while Stephanie steadied herself: The two squinted into the window. They could

just see the back of the hour hand, where an inscription was carved.

"Somebody better have a pencil!" Stephanie shouted. She read out the words she saw.

Well done! But it's neither here nor there.
For next an owl's hut needs repair;
Then seek a white raven, tangled in knots—
Only my heir can connect the dots.

"Perfect, Miss Knightleigh. I've got it!" said Nancy Weedle, writing in her notebook.

The teeth of the two gears began to close on Edgar's fingers, and Stephanie tried to swing back to the landing.

"Oh, no, you're taking me with you!" shouted Edgar, and he grabbed her foot just before the gears bit down on him. Stephanie yelped as the two swayed in midair, suspended only by her sweater.

"Mr. Glide! Mr. Glide!" cried Miles. "You can save them, just like you saved the nuclear acorn in *Squirrelman!*"

Blake Glide trembled as he looked down the dizzyingly high tower.

"Well, you know, that was a little different, since

I had sap blasters, and, uh, the insurance on my cheekbones doesn't kick in until next week, so . . ."

"Leggo! Leggo!" cried Stephanie, kicking her legs. "We're going to *faaaaaa . . .*"

The crowd shrieked as Stephanie's sweater ripped, and the two children plummeted toward the ground, ten stories below.

Whump.

Edgar slowly opened his eyes.

"'Whump'?" he said. "I expected 'splat.'"

"Not when the Volunteer Firefighter's Brigade is on the case," said Fire Chief Gully Lugwood. He and several firefighters held the canvas tarp they used to catch jumpers from burning buildings. (Of course, this was actually the first time they'd ever been able to use the tarp, since Nod's Limbsians always practiced proper fire safety rules and exited burning buildings from the designated fire escapes.) Gully Lugwood was ecstatic. "We weren't the first to catch the clue, but luckily, we caught you!"

Ellen raced down the stairs ahead of the crowd.

"Brother, you're still in one piece!" she said, giving him a relieved punch in the arm. She glanced at a dazed Stephanie, who was rubbing her head. "Drat. So is she."

14. Unsportsman-like Conduct

The Nod's Limbsians filed out of the clock tower, buzzing about the next riddle, but amid the speculations, some grumblings too could be heard.

"I think those children were trying to find that clue *without* the rest of us," said Arthur Poshi. "Flabbergasting!"

"*Children* wouldn't do such a thing," said Buffy. "Then again, Blake Glide himself snuck ahead of everyone to get the first clue, didn't he?"

"Do you get the feeling that not everyone is playing fair?" asked Betty LaFete.

Several people around them muttered and nodded.

"Did anyone stop to ask what we do when we *find* the limbs?" asked Marvin Matterhorn. "Are we going to sell them, and then split the money evenly? Give every team a gold finger or toe?"

The crowd seemed stumped by the idea. Finally, wax museum curator and custodian Ernest Hirschfeld spoke up. "Probably best to donate the limbs to the museum. That'd be the only fair thing . . ."

"You'd certainly benefit from that," said Marvin Matterhorn. "Tell me, Ernie, do you think that's what Blake Glide plans to do if he finds them first?"

Disagreements erupted from the group, and Principal Mulberry clapped her hands to silence the growing disquiet.

"Now, now, everyone," she called. "Where have all our happy faces gone? This riddle seems a little bit tougher, and we're going to need our very best teamwork to find the answer. We in the Teacher-Janitor Alliance have an idea about how to proceed next."

The principal outlined a plan for the teams to divide and explore an element of the clue. The words "owl" and "raven" seemed to point to the Nod's Limbs Zoo (even though the only birds on display were pigeons and chickadees), so the Silver Lining Ladies and the men of the Gauntlet would check that area first. To follow the clue about needing repairs, the Crosstown Contract Bridge Club and the Some-Quarter Pirates would check Greasy Billy's Gas Station and Mr. Chung's Cuckoo Clock Hospital. Several other teams were dispatched to shoe stores, Junior Nature Scout meeting dens, and the canoe dock to investigate "knots."

References to a "hut" were perplexing, since no one could recall such a structure in Nod's Limbs, but Team Gridiron volunteered to check the shopping mall. There, the food court boasted a Hamburger Hut *and* a Taco Hut—plus, there was the Kwik-Foto Hut in the parking lot and, for what it was worth, Sal's Fine China Hutch across the street. The Library Card League and the remaining teams were dispatched to seek reference to birds in town history and lore.

Blake Glide and the rest of the movie crew broke into teams of two or three, and left before Principal Mulberry could finish outlining her strategy.

"Great plan, everyone! Let's meet at town hall after dinner to go over our findings," said Principal Mulberry. "And remember: All for one and one for everybody!"

The teams tromped off to their assigned locations—though this time, Marvin Matterhorn, Arthur Poshi, and a few other Nod's Limbsians held back from the big groups. All of them had their excuses ("Paperwork piling up in the office," or "Hedges getting a little unruly"), but, curiously, not one of them left in the direction of his or her office or home.

15. Homophones Are Where the Heart Is

As the twins walked home through the forest, Ellen destroyed all the mushrooms in her path with punishing kicks.

"We're playing Nod's game," she said. "He's got us bumbling around just like the other goofballs in town."

Edgar strolled along with his head down and his hands clasped behind his back. He nodded slightly.

"We've got to get ahead of them, Brother," Ellen fumed. "We've got to break this next riddle before the rest of town does and take them *out* of the hunt. One thing's for sure, it's not at the zoo, because that's too easy—*Are you even listening to me?*"

Edgar looked up, startled. "Zoo, sure. Um, what were you saying?"

"Do you want to find those limbs or don't you? Concentrate, Edgar!"

Edgar stopped walking. "Wait. This . . . this may be nothing. Or maybe not. Where Nod is concerned, who knows?"

Ellen plopped onto a fallen pine and tugged a pigtail. "Let's hear it—even a half-wit's hunch will be better than anything those Nod's Limbsians come up with. I mean, zoos didn't even *exist* when Nod was alive. Imbeciles."

"Well, when Stephanie was reading the riddle, I got a look at it too. I noticed something that she didn't mention."

Ellen arched an eyebrow. "Go on."

"There were a couple of misspellings that, I don't know, just didn't feel very *Nod*. The first line read, 'Well done! But it's neither here nor there,'" said Edgar. "But *here* was spelled *h-e-a-r*, and *there* was *t-h-e-i-r*."

"Fairly common mistakes," said Ellen.

"Then the last line: *'Only my heir can connect the dots.' Heir* was spelled *a-i-r*."

Ellen snorted and mashed another toadstool into the dirt. "Okay. That's a little fishy."

"That's what I'm trying to tell you. Nod was a mad genius, right? He wouldn't make a careless mistake in his riddle unless he did it on purpose. To tell us something."

"Feh," muttered Ellen. She stood up and paced the thick brush and bramble of the Black Tree Forest. Then she turned and faced her brother.

"Hobophones," she said.

"What?" said Edgar.

"*Hobophones*. Words that sound the same but are spelled differently. Like *where* and *wear*. Or *Nod* and *gnawed*." She mimicked a fierce chewing motion. "What would Nod be trying to tell us by using hobophones?"

"I think you mean *homophone*," said Edgar.

"Whatever. But it *must* mean something," said Ellen. "I just can't figure it out—yet. I do know this: only *we* have this part of the clue."

"And Stephanie," Edgar pointed out. "She saw it too."

"Watch me tremble in my footies," said Ellen. "She probably didn't even notice the misspellings. And everyone else is following the wrong lead!"

16. Feed a Fever

When Edgar and Ellen put their minds to a problem, any number of things could happen. They might slip marsh-thistle spines into each other's bed sheets, or launch Pet from the broken bidet in the third-floor bathroom. Such activities often inspired their best ideas.

Today, however, they retreated to their own

corners to think—Ellen to the ninth-floor ballroom (which had a comforting clutter left behind by Judith Stainsworth-Knightleigh's home decoration failure) and Edgar to the parlor on the seventh floor, where he tootled half-heartedly on his out-of-tune pipe organ.

As the afternoon dragged by, Edgar gave up his absentminded music making, and climbed to the attic-above-the-attic for a change of scenery. There he aimed the twins' massive telescope at the town below to see how the other treasure hunters were faring.

Moments later he raced to the ballroom.

"Come on, Sister! You won't want to miss this!"

Ellen followed her brother down two floors to

the den, where Pet nestled on the couch. They had left the hairball there to enjoy its favorite pastime—watching nature documentaries on the old black-and-white TV set. But the show had ended hours ago, and because Pet no longer had the energy to change the channel, the little creature sat slumped miserably against a throw pillow watching *Antique Belt Buckle Showcase*.

"I got a look at something in the telescope. Something fun," said Edgar as he turned the dial to the Nod's Limbs Public Access Channel. Reporter Natalie Nickerson stood in the foreground. Behind her a mob of angry Nod's Limbsians accosted Blake Glide, who cowered from their shouts and shaking fists.

". . . which is why," Natalie Nickerson was saying, "these citizens are accusing movie megastar Blake Glide of foul play in the treasure-hunt craze that's sweeping town. Here's Ethel Elines, owner of the Hotel Motel. Mrs. Elines, can you tell our viewers what happened?"

Natalie pulled frail-looking Mrs. Elines by her elbow into the frame of the camera.

"Well, dear, it isn't my place to say a bad word about anyone, you understand," the old woman said. "But that handsome young man over there was actually digging out the bottom of our chicken coop. I believe he was even using my husband's shovel. Now our chickens are homeless and confused. What am I going to do?"

"There you have it, viewers," said Natalie Nickerson. "Blake Glide: coop raider, shovel thief. But he isn't the only one falling victim to gold fever. Our whole town seems gripped in its, uh, grip. Reports are coming in of shops closing unexpectedly, wandering bands of trowel-toting treasure hunters stopping traffic and crowding malls—and multiple incidents of neighbors digging in one another's yards *without permission.*"

A red-faced Chief Strongbowe leaned in and grabbed Natalie Nickerson's microphone. "Crushed pachysandra! Uprooted azaleas! Ravaged rhododendrons! My crack squad of gardeners won't stand for landscaping chaos. Lawn and Order will prevail!" He handed the microphone back to Natalie. "Ma'am."

"Madness," said the reporter. "Even my crew has abandoned their posts to go for the gold. I'm operating my own camera for this report! Now back to you in the studio, Barbara . . . Barbara? Are you there?"

Ellen turned off the TV. "Sweet little Nod's Limbs," she said. "Not so sweet these days, eh, Brother?"

"Nod predicted they'd dissolve into a greedy frenzy," said Edgar.

"While they're *dissolving*, we'll be solving." Ellen spread a piece of paper on the floor on which she had written the riddle.

> *Well done! But it's neither hear nor their.*
> *For next an owl's hut needs repair;*
> *Then seek a white raven, tangled in knots—*
> *Only my air can connect the dots.*

"Everyone else is only looking on the surface," said Ellen. "They see this bit about ravens and owls, and they think of zoos and chicken coops. But Nod's too clever to be so straightforward. Something is hiding here. Two phrases stand out to me: *needs repair* and *tangled in knots*."

"He's telling us something is broken," said Edgar. "We need to fix something. Or undo something."

"Or *unscramble* something," Ellen said.

Edgar sucked in a breath. "You mean . . . The thing that needs to be repaired isn't a *real* hut . . . it's the words themselves: *an owl's hut*!"

"Exactly. And there's no hog-tied bird anywhere in Nod's Limbs. It's the phrase *a white raven* we need to untangle!"

Edgar whooped and kicked his legs in the air. Even Pet seemed to bounce with joy. "Sister, that's brilliant! This is the closest I've ever come to wanting to hug you!"

"Thanks for resisting," said Ellen. "Now let's split up and do some unscrambling. You take the owl, I'll take the raven."

The twins sprawled on their bellies on the floor of the den with nubby pencils and scraps of paper, and began to rearrange the letters of the riddle.

It was simple enough to piece together gibberish phrases, but coming up with something that actually made sense proved more difficult. Edgar wrote and rewrote nonsense on the chance he would stumble across something. After what seemed like hours of scratching and erasing and half-mumbled cursing, he made his first discovery. The words "an owl's hut" could be reordered to spell "low haunts."

"What could be lower or more haunting than our basement?" he asked.

"No," his sister said. "Keep trying."

Edgar growled and hunched back over his sheet.

He muddled through a few more attempts (with Ellen rejecting "tuna howls," "Sultan Who," and his favorite: "oh walnuts") before arriving at two very promising leads.

"What do you think of 'town's haul' or 'south lawn'?" asked Edgar.

Ellen sat up. "Maybe it means both! The town's haul would be the golden limbs—and they're hiding in a south lawn somewhere."

"Did log cabins even *have* lawns in those days? Maybe he means Founder's Park," said Edgar. "Is that what your clue unscrambles to? It must!"

Ellen scowled. "I wish it would, but it's more stubborn than *you* are. So far 'a white raven' only gives us 'heavier want,' 'naïve wreath,' 'have tin-ware,' and, um . . . 'variant whee.'"

"Simple!" said Edgar, clapping his hands. "*Have tinware*. It's buried in a tin box in the southern half of Founder's Park. Grab a shovel, Sister, and let's get digging!"

"What about the homophone clue?"

"I don't know. Maybe there's a sign in Founder's Park we have to see first. It might point to the exact spot to dig."

"Hmm. It's worth a shot. What do you think,

Pet?" Ellen glanced at Pet, but its eye had shut and its tuft of hair lay flat.

"Ellen, we've got to hurry. Pet doesn't have long. We just need to dangle a golden pinkie or two in front of Eugenia's crew, and they'll get the spring dug out in no time. But first we need to find the limbs."

17. Sounds Like Victory

But the twins found that they were far from the first to search Founder's Park.

A hundred freshly dug holes dotted the lawn— south *and* north. Dozens of senior citizens with metal detectors (Team Golden Oldies) scoured the turf, listening for the faintest *ping* from their machines. After one white-haired gentleman in shorts and knee-high argyles heard such a beep, he flung down his detector and began digging.

"Ding-doggity!" he yelled. "Another bottlecap! When did the litterbugs take over our town?"

His teammates muttered curses without looking up from their work. The twins surveyed the scene in dismay.

"Did they unscramble the clue, too?" asked Ellen.

"I don't think so," said Edgar. "I think this town is really starting to lose it. They're just digging randomly now. Either way, they've already churned up the entire south lawn."

Ellen sat on the ground and groaned. "There's nothing buried here. Nothing! We're going to lose Pet . . . our house . . . everything!"

"No, no," said Edgar. "We were on the right track. I can feel it! Maybe 'have tinware' wasn't the right unscrambling—maybe there's another phrase we missed."

He took their paper scraps from his satchel and laid them out in front of him. As Team Golden Oldies

filed out of the park for dinner, Ellen joined her brother in poring over the jumble of letters.

"Bah! Fidgety little letters, getting all tangled up with one another."

But Edgar was obsessed. He scrawled on every inch of the paper, looking for every variation of the words.

"Good gravy, Sister, you've missed the most obvious one! *Whereat Ivan!* We just need to find this Ivan fellow and . . . Oh, wait. What about . . . Let's see, move the *H* . . . need this *A* . . . and another *A*, and . . . could it be? . . . YES!"

Edgar kissed the sheet of paper and did a celebratory cartwheel that landed him in one of the Golden Oldies' holes. He popped his head out of the pit and held out the paper for his sister to see. She peered at the list of words he had written, and at the bottom—right beneath "Ethan waiver"—she saw the words "weather vain!!!!"

"Wrong again, Edgar," said Ellen. "Weather *vane* is spelled *v-a-n-e* . . ." She gasped. "Homophones," she said. Now it was her turn to cartwheel. "The town's haul is in a weather vane! You're not as dumb as everyone says you are, Brother."

"I try," said Edgar, hopping out of the hole. "One problem, though. There must be hundreds of weather vanes around this town. Where do we begin?"

Ellen sat on the edge of the hole and thought about this a moment.

"It's not a haul we're after," she said. "It's a *hall*. As in—"

"Town Hall's weather vane!"

18. Sparring on the Spire

Nod's Limbs' stately Town Hall—another monument built during the Thaddeus Knightleigh era—loomed over Founder's Park directly to the east. In summer months, the building's dome enveloped Nod's statue in shadow from dawn to midmorning. Two hundred years ago, Thaddeus would regularly arrive at his office early just to enjoy the sight, which was, despite all his great public works, the only way he had ever been able to overshadow Augustus Nod in his lifetime.

Like all good town halls, a tall spire topped the domed roof, and, in turn, an ornate bronze weather vane topped the spire. And while most weather vanes depict a proud rooster—or perhaps a whale in coastal towns—Nod's Limbs' vane honored an entirely different creature: a bee, the humble insect whose wax had fueled the success of Nod's candle-making empire. After years of exposure to rain and snow, the glistening bronze bee had tarnished to a seasick green.

Edgar and Ellen sized up the leafy ivy that climbed to the roof.

"Exceedingly simple," said Edgar. "We climb up the ivy, you boost me onto the dome, I crawl up to the spire and check the weather vane."

"I boost you?" asked Ellen. "How about *you* boost *me*? It was my idea that cracked this whole thing wide open!"

"Your idea?" said Edgar. "Okay, smarty, last one to the top does the boosting."

The twins scrambled up the building, stepping on each other's fingers and jabbing at each other's eyes. Ellen reached the roof first (by head-butting her brother at the last second), and she sprawled atop the dome with a contented sigh.

"Ah, that was fun," she said.

She pulled Edgar up and the two took in the vista of the river and the seven covered bridges. When viewed from either end of town, the bridges bore jolly messages, one word per rooftop. Looking from the east end, they hailed, WELCOME FRIEND TO NOD'S LIMBS. STAY AWHILE, and from the west, COME BACK

SOON FRIEND AND TAKE CARE. From Town Hall's vantage point in the middle of town, the messages didn't make much sense when looking either direction; nevertheless, Edgar and Ellen knew those big, cheerful words by heart.

"Remember our carefree days when our only worries were how we were going to repaint the bridge messages?" Edgar asked.

"Ah, yes," recalled Ellen in a faraway voice. "GO AWAY NOW FOOL OR GET SCARRED."

"Who could forget FLEE MORTALS IT'S NOD'S LIMBS' ZOMBIE FEAST?" Edgar sighed. "Don't worry, Sister. We'll be back to our old ways soon, once our home is no longer threatened by Knightleighs. We just need to finish this hunt once and for all."

"Going up," said Ellen, waiting for her boost up the side of the dome. But then the twins heard a scraping, scrambling sound from the other side.

"Someone else is on the roof," whispered Ellen.

"Another treasure hunter?" asked Edgar softly.

Ellen held a finger to her lips, and they tiptoed around the perimeter. On the other side they encountered the one thing worse than a treasure hunter.

"You!" cried Ellen.

"You!" cried Stephanie Knightleigh.

Stephanie wore lavender mountain climber's boots and a bike helmet, and she held a rope that had been lassoed around the weather vane.

"Following us, eh, Knightleigh?" said Edgar. "Figures you would let our brains do all the work."

"I would never follow you," said Stephanie. "I couldn't stand being downwind."

"You noticed the misspellings too, then? And kept it to yourself?" said Ellen. "Sneaky, sneaky."

"Withheld information? Me? *Never*," she said with mock surprise. "I just assumed Nod was an idiot."

With that, she tightened her grip on the rope and sprang.

"She's going for the vane!" said Edgar, but Ellen was already in motion. As Stephanie scaled the dome, pulling herself up with the rope, Ellen caught the trailing rope behind her and followed. Stephanie saw her pursuer and raised her mountaineer's boot.

"Spikes!" yelled Ellen. She dodged the boot and managed to grab Stephanie's leg. Halfway up the side of the dome, the girls found themselves locked in an aerial wrestling match. They flailed, kicked, and shoved until the taut rope began to sway, sending them tumbling around the side of the dome like some sort of deadly maypole dance. As the two girls pitched back and forth, Edgar clambered past them on the rope, using their arms and legs as rungs.

"Get back here!" called Stephanie, grabbing at Edgar's arm. Edgar's leg caught in the rope, and the trio whomped and wailed at one another, trying to break free.

Suddenly a metallic squeak stopped them cold.

"That wasn't—" began Edgar.

"It was," yelped Ellen. The metal spire supporting the weather vane gave another sickening groan. They felt the rope twitch, and with a long *creeeeeeeeeeeak*, the spire bent nearly in half. The three combatants swung out over the side of the roof like fish on a hook. Beneath their toes, Edgar, Ellen, and Stephanie could see the steps of Town Hall waiting to catch them, a full four stories below.

Hardly daring to breathe they swayed back and forth with the steadfast rhythm of a clock pendulum, but the spire had stopped bending.

"Oh walnuts," said Edgar.

"Gnaw, Edgar," said Ellen. "Gnaw yourself out of these knots. Get the limbs and save Pet. If I've got to go, I can't think of a better person to go down with than the Purple Princess."

"Would you stop being so dramatic?" said Stephanie. "Besides, your body would totally break my fall."

But before Edgar could sink his teeth into the rope, he saw movement below.

"Oh no," he said. "I forgot! Principal Mulberry— she said everyone should meet—"

"At Town Hall after dinner!" said Ellen. "They'll find our clue!"

Indeed, clusters of Nod's Limbsians, having just polished off their dinners, were now trickling into the plaza in front of Town Hall.

"Maybe they won't notice us," said Ellen. "Everyone just act natural."

"Are you kidding?" said Stephanie. "I'm not cracking my head open for some dumb hunt. *Hellllp!*"

It was Fire Chief Gully Lugwood himself who climbed the fire engine ladder to cut them down.

"Well, you aren't white ravens, but you're certainly tangled in knots," he laughed. Then he got a closer look at his rescuees. "Oh. It's *you* two again. And . . . Miss Knightleigh! What on Earth . . . ?"

He gasped, then fixed them with an accusing glare. "You youngsters wouldn't be after another clue, would you?"

He was met with silence. He looked past the

three and saw the tarnished bee. Then Gully Lug-wood gave a curt nod to his crew below.

"I'm going to need a blowtorch," he called. "I think there's a lot more than three trespassing kids up here."

19. Face the Maestro

When Edgar and Ellen and Stephanie touched down at last, few citizens paid them any mind. All eyes were on the sheared-off weather vane being lowered to the ground after them.

"Curse you, Stephanie," said Ellen. "Thanks to you, the whole town gets the next clue *again*."

Stephanie didn't reply—she was watching her mother and father stride through the crowd.

"Daddy! Mother!" she called.

Judith Stainsworth-Knightleigh came close and replied in a low voice. "We distinctly told you to *avoid* attention. What do you call all of this?"

"The twins—" began Stephanie, but her mother cut her off with a wave of disgust. Her father looked as green as the weather vane.

The rest of the townspeople and scattered movie

crew gathered around as the Volunteer Firefighter's Brigade fiddled with the vane. At last Gully Lugwood uttered a triumphant "Aha!" as his penknife slipped inside a latch on the bronze bee's abdomen. The bee opened like a book, revealing a poem etched on its insides.

The fire chief read in silence for a moment, but after shouts from the crowd ("Share! Share!" and "Surely, it's your civic duty to read it to all!" and so on), he cleared his throat and read aloud:

> Now face the maestro, though it may howl.
> Foot it four furlongs and bring ye your trowel.
> Horseshoe hermit king and blue,
> As sixteen sees four, so must you too.

Not long ago, the treasure hunters would have speculated aloud, sharing their ideas about the riddle's solution. Now, only silence followed the reading of the clue.

Edgar and Ellen crouched low and whispered to each other.

"Face the maestro—is that Nod?" asked Edgar.

"Well, his statue is right across the street. It seems obvious, doesn't it?" said Ellen.

"Which can mean only one thing," said Edgar. "*That* isn't the answer."

Despite Edgar's assertion, most townsfolk lined up between Town Hall and the statue, facing due west as the riddle seemed to suggest. Remnants of the teams huddled together for hushed conferences. The twins strained to hear the whispered words.

"The maestro, the hermit king—it all points to Nod's statue. Is there another riddle hidden there?"

"No, no, it clearly said to walk four furlongs *past* the statue, and to bring a trowel. The next clue is buried!"

"Fine. What's a furlong?"

20. Mutiny

"Well, there's nothing about a horseshoe hermit king in here," said Ellen, slamming shut a book titled *Mane and Tail*. She and Edgar had returned to their house, but had come up with little more than theories for the solution to the clue.

They had looked in all kinds of books in their library, the biggest help coming from the dictionary's entry for "maestro": "a master, especially one who conducts an orchestra or teaches music." So far, though, the only musical footnote in town history was Willy Ach's All-Kazoo Barbershop Quartet, which had been a townwide rage in the early 1900s. Aside from that, nothing.

At one point Pet tried to get Ellen's attention by tickling her ear with a frizzled tendril, but Ellen was too absorbed in her research to notice. Eventually the creature leaned too far and rolled off Ellen's shoulder onto its own eyeball. After that, it napped fitfully on the dictionary stand. The twins were soon asleep as well.

As morning light spilled through the grimy windows, a familiar *twang-thump* sound came from downstairs, and the twins snapped awake.

"That was one of our traps!" said Edgar.

"The Wilhelm Screamer, from the sound of it," said Ellen. "Let's go!"

As the twins ran down the stairs, they found exactly what they had expected on the second-floor landing: a stuffed crocodile head, snout down, dangling from a set of ropes. The old beast had fallen from the ceiling and swallowed an intruder, whose sneakers jutted from the toothy maw.

"Thought you could sneak up on us, eh, Stephanie?" said Ellen. "Well, now you're gator fodder!"

"If it's Stephanie," said Edgar, sizing up the shoes, "she's shrinking."

"At ease, Wilhelm," said Ellen, hoisting the crocodile on creaky pulleys back into the air. Wilhelm spat out a quavering young pirate.

"Miles, what are you doing here?" cried the twins.

The boy straightened his feathered hat.

"I thought you might, um, be able to help me solve the clue," he said nervously.

"What's wrong with your little pirate buddies? Why aren't *they* helping you?" Edgar looked suspicious.

"They made me walk the plank," said Miles. "Calvin Hucklebee made himself captain of the Some-Quarter Pirates since he solved the first clue— or he says he solved it, at least. But I'm the one who knows everything about pirates."

"What do you need from us, Miles? Make it quick," said Ellen.

"I had an idea, but Calvin wouldn't listen, and neither will my family," said Miles. "I remember reading something in an old pirate comic about the word *maestro*. It was issue 77, or maybe 78, of 'Captain Bloodgut of the Barbary Coast,' but last year my mom threw all my comics away—"

"We don't have any comics, Miles," said Ellen.

"That's okay. Stephanie told me once you had a really big room full of maps. Maps are what I need."

"Maps," said Ellen. "Sure. Knock yourself out. But"—she blocked his way—"you have to tell us everything you find out."

Miles nodded. Ellen started to lead the way to the map room when Edgar grabbed her elbow and pulled her aside.

"Are you out of your lumpy skull?" he hissed. "Why are you letting him use our resources?"

Ellen only sucked her teeth.

"He's one of *them*," continued Edgar. "If he discovers something—and that's a big *if*—he'll blab it to everyone. And in case you've forgotten, *he's a Knightleigh!*"

Ellen spun on her brother and whispered, "First of all, we haven't had a bright idea all night. In case *you've* forgotten, we're racing against time. I'd team up with a dirty sock if it would help save Pet. And second of all . . ."

Ellen's voice trailed off. The twins had an unspoken agreement never to mention the frightful days when Ellen had been under a personality-altering trance and had unwittingly attended a particularly cruel slumber party at Stephanie's. The other girls had behaved unspeakably to Ellen, and the only one who didn't make fun of her—the only one who had shown her any kindness—had been Miles Knightleigh.

"It's just, well, Miles isn't so bad," said Ellen at last. Edgar goggled, but kept his mouth shut.

21. A Bad Day for Mr. Frimmel

Miles pored over rolls of yellowed paper, unfurling each map carefully and examining it.

"What exactly are you looking for?" asked Edgar. "A way out of this town?"

"No, silly," said Miles. "I know where that is. No, it's something Captain Bloodgut said when the Corsican She-Devil attacked his ship."

"Do tell," said Edgar.

"Well, when the Corsican She-Devil appeared out of nowhere off the starboard bow of the *Squawking Parrot*, Captain Bloodgut said something about a 'malevolent maestro' bringing her there. And I just had a hunch. . . ."

"Comics," said Edgar, rolling his eyes. "What *can't* they teach us?" He slid out of his chair and left to go watch TV, mumbling that he'd found more interesting things when plucking nose hairs.

Pet lay in Ellen's lap, shivering. Ellen regarded Miles skeptically as he unfurled another map (OVERLAND TRADE ROUTES FOR NORTHERN NOVA SCOTIA) and quickly rolled it back up.

"Why does your cat have only one eye?" asked Miles.

"It lost a fight with a giant sloth," said Ellen.

"Neat," he said. "Hey, did you hear what happened last night? Everybody walked west for four furlongs—turns out that's half a mile—and then they were at 1604 West Florence Boulevard. You know, Mr. Frimmel's store? The Clarinet Emporium? Well, everybody saw the sixteen and the four, just like the riddle, and it made them a little nutsy and they tore up Mr. Frimmel's store! They didn't find anything, but I knew they wouldn't. People have been digging up and down the street all night. They're like crazy dogs. Or squirrels. Squirrels dig holes too sometimes. I've seen it—Ooh! Ooh! I found it! I found it!" cried Miles, leaning over a map of the Mediterranean Sea. "'Maestro' means—"

"Forget it," said Edgar, slouching into the room. "The limbs have been found. We've lost."

22. The Mayor Victorious

The twins wanted Pet to rest at home, but the creature wouldn't let Edgar close his satchel without being tucked inside. The twins and Miles ran all the way to Nassau Way, where it seemed everyone in town had gathered outside a long, low building. Two hundred years ago, this old building had been the Nod's Limbs Livery Stable, where citizens rented horses and carriages of the finest quality. Today it was still a stable, though its only regular inhabitants were cranky old Mr. Bundersen, the stable master, and cranky old Gertie, the mare who pulled the hayride wagons each Falling for Fall Festival.

Mayor Knightleigh stood outside of the stables next to a cartful of golden arms and legs. He basked in the glory of the TV camera lights as he spoke into Natalie Nickerson's microphone.

"So then I realized Nod wasn't referring to *himself* as the maestro, he was referring to my late ancestor, Thaddeus Knightleigh, who of course lived down this street in stately Knightleigh Manor. So when you face northeast from town hall and walk a half-mile toward the manor, you arrive here at the stables!"

Miles fumbled with the handful of maps he had brought with him. "Aw, gee, I was so sure I was right," he said glumly.

The mayor continued. "When I saw the stable, I said to myself, 'Mr. Mayor, you may be a clever and handsome man, as well as a great civic leader, but what about the rest of the clue?' You will be relieved to know I had an answer for myself. I said, 'Self, this is where the *horseshoes* were, the very ones used by Nod, the *hermit king,* on his horse whose name, legend has it, was Old *Blue.*'"

"I thought it was Clip-Clop," said Ernest Hirschfeld.

"No, no. Definitely *Old Blue.* Lo and behold when I looked in the fourth aisle, inside the sixteenth stable, what did I find behind a loose board but these very precious limbs, thus ending our hunt and making me the legitimate owner of all Nod's possessions, which I can assure you, was only these limbs."

The mayor beamed, but he seemed to be the only one excited about the news. A few citizens (and at least one major motion picture star) wept openly.

"You all will be happy to hear that, through the good will of me, I am donating these limbs to the Nod's Limbs Museum of Wax. Now, I know they're not strictly wax, but it will be nice to see them on display and remember what fun we had looking for them and how generous I am. Bob!"

Bob, the mayor's intern, stepped forward.

"Cart these keepsakes to the museum, Bob!" said the mayor. "As for the rest of you, go on home and get back to your normal, non-gold-hunting lives. Bye-bye, now!"

The crowd began to wander away.

"I can't believe Knightleigh outsmarted us," said Edgar, clenching his fists. He turned on Miles. "You were sent to throw us off track, weren't you?"

"I wasn't! I did it on my own!" said Miles. "Um, that's not what I mean. I mean I was on the right track, I just know it!"

"It just doesn't seem fair," said Miss Croquet. "He already has so much."

"Museum? Ha! If I didn't win them, I don't want to *look* at them," said Marvin Matterhorn. "My family is boycotting the Museum of Wax from now on."

"Come, Sir Geoffrey," said a saddened Sir Malvolio. "Hence! I am mistempered by our defeat in this folly for gold—"

"I know that gold!" blurted Sir Geoffrey, pointing at the limbs. "That's our paint, Malvolio! *Mead Gold!*"

The senior Gallant Paintsman cast a glance at the cart, tilted his head curiously, and then moved in for a closer look.

Mayor Knightleigh stepped in front of Sir Malvolio and held up his hand. "Move along now, *sirs*. Surely a garage somewhere needs a fresh coat of paint."

"Beg pardon, my lord." Sir Malvolio pushed past the mayor, "But methinks Sir Geoffrey speaks true!"

"Darn tootin' I speak true!" Sir Geoffrey raced to the cart and picked up one of the legs. "I had Mead Gold in my hair for weeks after that crazy girl in pajamas flipped out on Mrs. Stainsworth-Knightleigh's show!"

The mayor stormed after Sir Geoffrey. "Drop my leg, painter!"

Upon hearing the commotion, the townspeople began to gather again.

"Doesn't weigh much for pure gold!" Sir Geoffrey tossed an arm to Sir Malvolio.

Heidi Birchbeer grabbed the other arm from the cart and scratched it with a fingernail. Gold paint flecks fell to the ground. "The—the limbs aren't gold! This *is* paint!"

"Great hog!" Lyman Herringbottle held the final limb aloft. "This leg is wood!"

"Nod buried wooden limbs?" asked Betty LaFete. "This was all a hoax?"

"A hoax indeed, madam," said Mr. Herringbottle, "but not by Nod. This paint is new."

"Aye. Whilst the quality of our paint is legendary," boasted Sir Malvolio, "it has been to market nary a decade!"

"That's right!" shouted Sir Geoffrey, shaking an arm at the mayor. "Someone here has planted *fake limbs*!"

The mayor looked stunned.

"You—you mean, I've been *had*?" he asked. "That, well, that seems unsporting, don't you think? I shall launch a full investigation to ferret out the guilty party, but until such time, perhaps we should postpone the search—"

"The hunt is back on!" shouted Chief Strongbowe.

The townspeople's sorrowful faces turned jubilant.

"We can still find the *real* gold limbs!"

"But who planted the fake ones?"

Neighbors eyed one another warily, but one thing was for sure: *Someone* was not playing fair. The citizens of Nod's Limbs rushed away as quickly as they had gathered, desperate to find the next clue.

Edgar leaped in the air.

"I knew it! I knew that melon-headed mayor could never outwit us!" he shouted. "Now what do we do?"

"Batten down your hatches and follow me!" said Miles.

23. Thar's a Fair Wind A-Blowing

"Are you sure about this?" asked Edgar. They had returned to Town Hall with the old maps Miles had carried from the twins' house. Edgar glanced around, checking for spies.

"I'm double-triple sure," said Miles. "I *knew* I knew what Captain Bloodgut meant! Pirates in the old days, they had names for each of the winds. That way, when the wind blew, they wouldn't say something boring, like, 'The wind's coming from the south.' They would say something much more awesome, like, ''Tis a cruel sirocco blowin' trouble our way, an' no mistake.'"

Miles smoothed a map on the ground. The map depicted the coastline of the Mediterranean Sea as well as curving lines and arrows showing channels, reefs, common wind conditions, and other notations for the savvy sailor.

In the lower right the map bore the customary compass pointing the way to north, south, east, and west. Just as Miles had said, each point of the compass had a word written beside it naming a wind. To the south, 'sirocco'; to the southeast, 'marin'; to the north, 'mistral'; to the west, 'zephyros'; and to the northwest—

"Maestro!" cried the twins together.

"Miles, you're a black-hearted, red-bearded, hook-handed genius!" said Ellen.

"And don't ye be fergettin' it," said Miles. *"Arrrr."*

He unfurled another parchment, this one the old map of Nod's Lands that had been tacked to the wall of the map room. "Okay, so we just look on this map and see what's four furlongs northwest of Town Hall."

But it wasn't quite that easy. The map didn't have a scale, and furthermore, that quadrant of the map showed nothing but forest.

"We better get exploring," said Edgar.

"But we can't waste our time walking all over town," Ellen protested, snatching the map.

"I've got an idea," said Miles, taking off his shoe.

"Not all over town, Sister. Just northwest," said Edgar.

"No, really, I think I've got it," said Miles.

"Ah, yes, good thing northwest is only a quarter of the whole town," Ellen replied. "Miles, put your shoe back on."

Miles sighed and grabbed the map from Ellen.

"Hey!" she exclaimed as Miles spread his shoelace across the parchment.

"I bet it's here," he said, pointing. "My shoelace says so."

"Oh, well, why didn't we ask the shoelace in the first place?" snapped Edgar.

"No, look. See?" said Miles. "I used my shoelace to measure the distance between Town Hall and the corner of Florence and Fifth—Mr. Frimmel's store. That was four furlongs, right? So I use that same length to go from Town Hall toward the maestro. . . ."

The end of the shoelace fell right at the base of Nod's Limbs historic Crabby Apple Tree.

"We could have done that," Ellen snorted, wagging a footie in the air. "But we don't care much for shoelaces."

24. The Root of the Problem

The three headed across the river toward Cairo Avenue and the Crabby Apple Tree.

"Where do you suppose we start?" Edgar asked as they walked. "I don't see a horseshoe factory or a hermit king's house. I guess we case it now, and come back at night for further exploration."

Ellen scanned the street in both directions. Cairo Avenue was lined on both sides with pretty Victorian houses in pastel blues and yellows. Manicured lawns and evenly trimmed hedges acted as a buffer between the homes and bustling Cairo Avenue. Just ahead of them, a spindly crabapple tree grew in the middle of the street.

The Crabby Apple Tree was said to be where Nod first tied his horse when he arrived in the desolate forest that was to become Nod's Limbs. The tree was so beloved that future generations preferred to split traffic *around* it rather than cut it down. Edgar stared at the tree and chewed his lip. All of a sudden, he hollered, "Criminy! The Crabby Apple Tree, Sister! Don't you see? Horseshoe! Hermit! King! Blue! Those are all kinds of *crabs!*"

"*Shh!*" hissed Ellen. "I mean, that's brilliant, but still—*shh!*"

"We're the best!" Miles whisper-yelled.

"It all makes sense!" said Edgar. "'As sixteen sees four'—four is sixteen's square *root!*"

"Yay!" said Miles. "What's a square root?"

"Who cares?" said Ellen. "Come nightfall, it's time to dig!"

"So the scent's hot again, is it, kids?" said a voice behind the hedges. Don Pickens stood up holding a pair of hedge clippers. "I'll help you dig. We won't have to tell anyone else about it."

"Tell anyone else what?" said a man in the next yard over.

"Crud," said the twins.

"Oh no you don't, Johnson!" cried Don Pickens to his neighbor. "You just want the gold for yourself!"

The bickering gathered the attention of motorists and other neighbors. As the word "gold" floated over Cairo Avenue in the middle of a sunny Sunday afternoon, restraint and cordiality melted like a double-decker ice cream cone in a hothouse.

The twins and Miles watched helplessly as hordes of citizens attacked the dirt around the Crabby Apple Tree. With no more to go on than "it's in the roots," treasure hunters grabbed shovels and hoes from nearby gardens and burrowed holes on all sides of the trunk, flinging clods of dirt into one another's faces. Soon the ground was as pocked as a rotten sponge. At last Mr. Pickens heard a *thunk* under his spade, and the frenzy stopped.

There was no concealing the find. The townspeople tensed with anticipation as Mr. Pickens unearthed a rusty metal box. It was so corroded that the lid fell off when he touched it. He gingerly pulled an old scrap of paper from inside and was forced to read it aloud:

> *There and back and there again.*
> *To find the limbs, now seek Nod's friend.*

The riddle's perched above the floor,
By one, then two, then three, then four.

Sated by the new riddle, the hopeful hunters quickly retreated, each off to crack the riddle on his or her own.

After the twins and Miles—the last to leave—trudged away, a cool maestro blew over Cairo Avenue. With most of its roots exposed to the sky, the beloved Crabby Apple Tree swayed in the breeze, toppled, and split in two.

25. The Blackest Hour

Since Miles was expected home for dinner, the twins returned to their house alone. Pet rode on Ellen's shoulder until a slight breeze blew a clump of the creature's hair onto the road. After that they put Pet in Edgar's satchel. Edgar kicked the dirt as they walked along.

"Sister . . . are we wasting our time with the hunt? Would we have been better off down in the cavern, digging out the spring?"

"No telling how far we could have gotten," said

Ellen. "Meanwhile Pet gets worse and worse . . . and our doomed house . . ."

They walked in silence for some time. At last Edgar said something so unexpected it made Ellen grimace.

"I wonder where our parents are," he said.

In all the years since their parents had disappeared, leaving a note saying they had gone on extended holiday, neither Edgar nor Ellen had ever actually wondered out loud about them.

Ellen took a long time to respond. "Do you think things would have turned out . . . differently if they were here now?"

"*Differently*, sure," said Edgar. "It's *better* that I wonder about."

Ellen grunted. "Look what having parents did for Stephanie. I want Heimertz back. He cared about Pet . . . and us."

"If anybody could have dug out the spring, it was him. And who would dare knock down this house with a caretaker like *that* protecting it?" Edgar paused. "But I don't think he's coming back, Sister."

"I guess he never got our note," said Ellen, dropping her head into her hands. "Now there's no one to help us but *us*." After a moment she looked up again. "I'd give up everything to save Pet."

Edgar nodded. "But what's the better way to do it? Solve a madman's riddle or go back to shoveling out the balm?"

"If we go back to the caves, we'd need to devise a way of digging faster," said Ellen. "Some method of moving large amounts of earth."

"Sort of like the way those townies tore into the Crabby Apple Tree," said Edgar. "We need an army of people like that."

Ellen pulled her pigtails. "Yes . . . yes. An army like that. How do you suppose we could convince a large number of people to come to our house and dig in a frantic frenzy?"

"Oh no—no more riddles," said Edgar.

"Oh *yes*—we just need a riddle of our own," said Ellen. "We have to convince the Nod's Limbsians that *the golden limbs are buried at our house*."

Edgar smiled a crooked smile. "I see, I see. If they

thought Nod's treasure was hidden, say, *in our cavern* . . . right beneath the cave-in . . . Why, they would shovel themselves crazy to get to the bottom, wouldn't they?"

"That they would, Brother!" said Ellen. "We just need to plant a fake riddle that points to our house, and the locals will come flocking with their shovels. We'll uncover the balm in hours, not days!"

"Which means we need to solve this *Nod's friend* thing first, so we can plant *our* riddle in its place," said Edgar.

Pet nuzzled Edgar's hand.

"Hang onto your follicles, Pet," he said. "We're going to save you yet!" And the rest of the way home, the twins sang:

> *Make them think the gold is under*
> *This gray house and they'll come plunder,*
> *Tear the very ground asunder—*
> *That greedy, grasping group.*
> *Digging, digging, ever deeper,*
> *'Midst the crawlies and the creepers,*
> *Find a secret spring and keep our*
> *Pet off Death's front stoop.*

26. In the Blink of an Eye

"Nod's friend . . . Nod's friend." Edgar paced back and forth. "Nod didn't have any friends! He was a miserable old codger who died lonely and poor!"

The twins had turned their den into a sort of war room with reference books piled everywhere, maps covering the walls, and Natalie Nickerson blathering away on the TV, keeping them informed of breakthroughs (or the lack thereof) in the outside world. After some debate they had decided that the line "seek Nod's friend" could have but a single meaning. While the old hermit seemed to have no friends in the human realm, his journal made it clear that he did have one trusted companion: a certain fuzzy, one-eyed hairball seated before them. The twins had tried to extract information from Pet about Nod, his habits, his acquaintances, and had even given the creature a pencil so it could make some of the doodles it used to communicate.

But Pet was too weak to write legibly, and it had grown frustrated and crabby. It seemed to lose more hair every time it moved, and it finally let the pencil fall and closed its eye tight. Now it lay in a bundle of rags the twins had piled together as a little nest.

"Looking worse than ever," sighed Ellen.

"Which?" asked Edgar glumly. "Pet? Or our chances of finding the limbs?"

"Both," said Ellen. "At least with the other clues I had some idea of where to begin. Now, our only lead may go from dead *end* . . . to *dead*."

At this, Pet's eye popped open. The creature gazed at Ellen and quivered.

"Uh, the *deadline* you mean . . . for solving the clue . . ." Edgar elbowed his sister in the ribs.

"Right, of course," said Ellen. "Ugh, I just *wish* Nod's journal hadn't gone up in flames."

"If only I'd read the passages more carefully," said Edgar. "But we were just interested in the balm and Pet. And there wasn't much in there, either. Mostly scientific jargon."

"Still, I don't recall any mention of him having dinner guests, sending fruit baskets, or mailing out holiday cards," said Ellen.

"Or he didn't write about it, if he did," said Edgar. "I mean, the only *friend* of Nod's that we know of is—"

"Pet. I know. But Pet can't tell us anything, Brother."

Pet blinked.

"There's got to be a way!" said Edgar. "A way to communicate. *Something*."

"Look at it, Edgar! It can barely blink—" Ellen stopped. "Wait! That's it!"

"What?"

"Pet." Ellen dropped her head down, so it was level with the hairball. "We're going to ask you some yes or no questions. Do you think you can blink the answers? Once for yes, twice for no."

Pet blinked, albeit slowly.

"Okay, Edgar, what should we ask it? We should try to make this quick—I think even blinking takes its toll."

"Pet, did Nod have any friends besides you?" asked Edgar.

Pet blinked twice.

"That's what I thought! So, where do we go from there?"

"Maybe we're getting too caught up on the 'Nod's friend' bit. There *are* three other lines to the clue."

"True, but the fact that the next clue is 'perched above the floor' doesn't give us a whole lot to go on."

Both the twins were pacing now, trying to think of the right question to ask.

"Okay, what do we know?" said Ellen. "Nod was

a hermit. He didn't have anybody in his life. . . ."

Pet shifted as much as it was able, but the twins didn't notice.

"And he died penniless, except for this house—"

Pet shuddered so hard, it fell out of its nest. This got the twins' attention.

"What? What is it, Pet?"

Pet blinked twice.

"No? What do you mean?"

Pet's eye closed and stayed that way. It could do nothing more.

"Wait, Ellen, what was the last thing you just said?"

"That Nod died penniless."

Pet blinked. Twice.

"Nod *wasn't* penniless when he died?"

Pet blinked twice, and looked expectantly from one twin to the other.

Ellen pulled a pigtail. "Nod was rich when he died?"

One blink.

"Very rich?"

This time, Pet blinked four times, just for emphasis.

Edgar frowned. "So Herringbeetle was wrong. What does it matter anyway?"

"You dunderhead—don't you see? Everyone thought Nod was penniless, because he lived alone in the woods and didn't leave a will. If Nod *was* wealthy when he died, where did it all go? Money, possessions, land—it had to go into *someone's* hands. What if whoever has it, is this 'friend' in the riddle?"

"But where are we going to look? We're already on one treasure hunt—I don't fancy starting another one with even fewer clues."

"What about a safe bet?" said Ellen, grinning. "And when I say 'safe,' I mean it literally." She pointed to a map of Nod's Limbs—the corner of Florence and Sydney. Though few modern landmarks existed on the 200-year-old map, there was one in particular that had stood the test of time: the Nod's Limbs Bank.

"Safety deposit boxes, Brother," said Ellen. "The little vaults in banks where people keep their most cherished secrets locked away. Maybe Nod left some clues there for us to find."

27. Break-In

"Typical," said Edgar. "Nod's Limbsians make breaking and entering no fun at all."

It was a little after midnight, and he and Ellen were crouched outside the bank beside an unlocked basement window. Ellen swung it open as Edgar put his crowbar back into his satchel with a disappointed sigh. The twins crawled into the room, where private lockboxes lined every wall.

"At least I'll get a little practice with my lock pick," said Edgar, lighting up the room with a flash-

light. "We sent my best one to Heimertz, but I have a hand-sharpened hairpin I've been itching to try."

Ellen nudged her brother and pointed to a big sign on the wall:

FORGET YOUR KEY? NO PROBLEM! USE MINE.
(DON'T FORGET TO PUT IT BACK!)
—BECKY FAFF, PRESIDENT, NOD'S LIMBS BANK

A nail next to the sign held a single key on a colorful lariat.

"This town is so *infuriating*," Edgar groaned. "It's like we're living inside a sugar cube."

"Come on, they're all alphabetical, so this shouldn't take long," said Ellen. She grabbed the key. "If there's no Nod, we scram."

"I can't believe we haven't discovered this room before now," said Edgar, eyeing the rows upon rows of lockboxes. "Some of these date back to the 1700s—centuries worth of skeletons in closets, all at our disposal!"

"Look, here are the *N*s," said Ellen. She and Edgar started reading names off the labels.

"Needermeyer . . . Neferhausen . . . Nickerson . . . Nopworst . . . No, I don't see a Nod."

"Blast!" cried Ellen. "I felt *so sure* we'd find something here."

Ellen leaned her head against the boxes in frustration.

"Come on, Ellen, we're wasting time."

"But I just know there's something we're missing!" She looked at the boxes in front of her, trying to think of what to do next, when one of the names caught her eye.

"Edgar! Look!"

The way the boxes were shelved, the *K*s fell directly above the *N*s. Edgar followed Ellen's gaze and gasped.

"A. Nod Knightleigh."

28. Keep Your Enemies Close

"It—it can't be Augustus, right?" Ellen finally asked. "He wasn't actually a *Knightleigh*, was he?"

Ellen put the master key in the lock, and gave it a turn. The mechanism resisted at first, as if two centuries of dust had jammed the inner workings. But with a gritty, grinding sound, the lock clicked. The twins held their breath as Ellen slid the box open.

Just then they heard someone fumbling with the door. The twins froze—they were in the middle of the room with nowhere to hide. Becky Faff was obviously a trusting soul, but even she would probably be suspicious to find the twins alone in the dark, breaking into a Knightleigh's lockbox.

The door swung open. The twins could see a silhouette of a person, but it didn't look quite tall enough to be the bank manager. In fact, it bore a resemblance to—

"Stephanie!" cried Ellen.

"What? Who's there?" Stephanie Knightleigh looked around frantically as Edgar shone his flashlight at her.

At first it looked like she was dressed in all black, down to her black boots and black gloves, and a black ski mask pulled up to her brow, but then the twins realized that the color was actually a deep eggplant. When Stephanie saw the twins, she dropped the duffel bag she was carrying.

"You two!"

"Felon!" said Edgar. "We caught you *red-handed*, Stephanie! You broke into the bank!"

"*I'm* the felon?" said Stephanie, regaining her composure. "You broke in first! I've caught you with your hand in someone's lockbox! Just wait till I tell my father!"

"Just wait till we tell the whole town!" Ellen shot back. She grabbed Stephanie's mask off her head. "This doesn't look like deposit apparel."

Stephanie glared at the twins, and the twins glared right back, and no one said anything for several seconds. Finally Stephanie broke the silence.

"Okay, so we both had the same idea," said Stephanie, "Now what'd you find?"

"Like we're going to tell *you*," Ellen spat.

"You tell me, or I have you arrested." Stephanie whipped out her purple cell phone.

"You're bluffing!" Ellen hissed. "You'd be in just as much trouble as—"

"As what? *You* two?" Stephanie asked with smirk. "Tell me, whose father is the most powerful man in town?"

Ellen scowled, but Edgar touched her elbow. "She's right. We don't have much of a choice. Nobody would believe us over a Knightleigh." He leaned into her ear and whispered, "And we can always sabotage her after we get out of here."

"Fine. We'll"—Ellen choked a little—"compromise."

Stephanie grabbed her mask back from Ellen. "Okay, rules. One: While we're in this bank, we truce—no stealing, no smuggling, no dupes. Agreed?"

The twins nodded, though Ellen's face still looked like she'd eaten a bushel of lemons.

"Two: We share *all* information, and can use it as we please."

The twins consented.

"And three: We don't tell *anyone* what we find here."

"Done," said Ellen. "Now will you let us get back to spying? You're about as stealthy as a garbage truck."

"And you smell like one. Now, what have we got?"

Ellen reluctantly stepped out of the way, and Stephanie saw the name on the lockbox.

"That's Knightleigh property! As a descendent, whatever's in that box belongs to me!"

"Ah, ah, ah," said Ellen. "Share all information, remember?"

29. The Lockbox

Whether the twins and Stephanie expected to find rolls of bank notes, another miniature golden statue, or even further clues to the hunt, they were all disappointed. The sole contents of the lockbox were a small stack of unopened letters and a heart-shaped locket.

Stephanie reached for the locket, but Ellen grabbed it first and opened it. Inside were two inked drawings. They were very old, the kind drawn in the days when no one smiled for portraits. A man and a woman gazed up at them. Even though neither of them smiled, they made a handsome couple.

The man was clean shaven, with wavy dark hair and an aquiline nose. The woman also had dark features, but for her large, light eyes. Despite her beauty there was a distinct sadness about those eyes.

"Who's the guy?" asked Ellen. "Nod?"

"Doesn't look much like the statue," said Edgar.

"So who do you think it is?"

Stephanie snatched up the locket.

"Don't you dare pocket that," warned Ellen.

"I wasn't going to," Stephanie retorted. "Everyone knows that you always put an inscription on a locket. See?" She pulled a gold chain out from beneath her collar. On it was a K-shaped locket with the inscription:

To Stephanie,

The sun shines more brightly when you're a Knightleigh.

Love,
Mother and Daddy

Ellen rolled her eyes.

"Now, let's see," Stephanie examined the back of the old locket. "Yes, look: 'To my sweet Agatha, with all my love, Pierre.'"

"Putrid," said Edgar.

Stephanie didn't say anything. She had started to look a little uncomfortable.

Edgar turned his attention to the letters. "Hey, these are addressed to Augustus," he said, sifting through them. "But they're all returned to sender. Mrs. Pierre Knightleigh. These must be portraits of Pierre Knightleigh and his wife, Agatha."

"So *A* stands for Agatha, not Augustus," said Ellen. "But why the 'Nod'? Unless—"

"No! It can't be!" shouted Stephanie. Edgar dropped some of the letters at the outburst.

"What's the matter with you?" asked Ellen.

Stephanie clutched her ancestor's locket so tightly her knuckles turned white.

"Pierre Knightleigh was the son of Thaddeus Knightleigh, Nod's Limbs' first mayor."

"So?"

"So, as every Knightleigh knows, Pierre married Babette Croquet, and they had a son, Haggis Knightleigh—"

"They named their kid after sheep guts?" asked Ellen.

"Apparently it was fashionable at the time," huffed Stephanie. "Look, the important thing is, *Pierre and Babette* continued the Knightleigh lineage. He was never married to any *Agatha!*"

"I still don't see what the big deal is," said Edgar as he opened the top letter. He perused the contents and let out a long, low whistle.

"What does it say?" asked Ellen and Stephanie in unison.

"You're not going to believe this," said Edgar, and he began to read aloud:

To my dearest father—

I am writing for the last time.
You yet refuse to answer my letters,

and no one has heard from or seen you in months. It is of the utmost importance that you show yourself, or at least make known your existence.

Since Thaddeus' death and burial in the Knightteigh tomb, his widow has been calling for an inquiry into your own whereabouts. Father, she wants to declare you dead! I do not believe that you are—in my heart, I know that you are alive somewhere, though whether you have departed our fair town forever I cannot fathom.

Still, you must be aware of the consequences of your absence. Without a legal will bequeathing all your many possessions, the widow Knightteigh will insist that I, as your only child, inherit everything—not just your monetary wealth, but the Waxworks, the acres of forest, the house, and <u>what lies beneath the house</u>, will all pass to my husband—and thus the rest of the Knightteigh family.

I love Pierre, but his mother is not to be trusted. She is cruel and possessive, and she wields a power over Pierre that I cannot break. I am afraid of what corruption might arise should the Life Balm come into her hands. And what of dear Pilosoculus? She would stuff its little eyeball and display it on her mantle like some kind of trophy!

I cannot prevent this if you do not come forward. I grow weaker by the day, and I do not know how much longer I will survive the sickness inside. I know you feel I have betrayed you by marrying the son of your enemy, but still am I committed to protecting you and the secret of the balm, for the good of all.

Please, papa, forgive me. I miss you, and love you,

Your Agatha

Edgar folded the letter and stuck it back in its envelope.

"So Nod had a daughter," he said.

"And since she married Thaddeus' son, all the Nod wealth passed to the Knightleighs," said Ellen. She and Edgar both looked at Stephanie, who had taken several steps backward into the darkness. Her skin was ashen.

"I—I didn't know," she said, almost to herself. "Why didn't Daddy tell me?"

A thought struck Ellen.

"Your father! He was the only one insisting that Nod died penniless. But he knew! He knew that if no one ever found a will, the Knightleighs could keep Nod's money forever!"

"But now there *is* a will," said Edgar, "and it clearly states that all of Nod's possessions go to the person who solves the hunt. It's not just the limbs anymore. . . ."

"It's everything," said Stephanie bitterly. The shock in her eyes had turned to fiery anger, but when she spoke, her voice was like ice cracking. "You're loving this, aren't you? Someone finds the golden limbs, and lucky ducky gets the Knightleigh fortune to boot, all because of a stupid technicality."

She threw the locket back in the box and slammed it shut. "You think you'll be the ones? I can promise you this: No one will get a single cent from us, limbs or no limbs!"

30. Back to the Dart Board

The twins went straight home after leaving the bank. Pet was still curled up in its nest in the den. Patches of its hair had whitened even while the twins were away, and it didn't wake as they entered.

"The Knightleighs are about to lose everything," said Edgar. "Even better, they're going to lose it to *us*."

"But no one can find out about this, not until we have the limbs in our possession," said Ellen. "Can you imagine how crazy people would get if they knew the extent of the inheritance?"

"We just have to solve this clue first," said Edgar. He pulled it out again and looked at it for the hundredth time. "I just don't get it. There's something we're missing. Ellen—stay focused, will you?"

Ellen had picked up some darts and begun tossing them at the old map of Nod's Limbs on the wall.

She ignored her brother as she pulled the darts out of the map and threw them again.

"Something we're missing . . ." she muttered.

Thwack.

"Something so simple . . ."

Thwack.

"We've overlooked it completely. . . ."

Thwack. Ellen looked at the dart she had just thrown. It had landed on one of the covered bridges. The center one.

The Cairo Avenue bridge.

"Brother! Brother, I think I've got it!" she yelped, running to the map. Edgar looked up from his doodlings, startled.

"What is it?"

"Look!" Ellen grabbed his pencil and wrote, from west to east, on the bridges' roofs, "Welcome Friend to Nod's Limbs. Stay Awhile," and from east to west, "Come Back Soon Friend and Take Care."

"The middle bridge . . . ," Edgar gasped.

There were two words written on the roof of the Cairo Avenue bridge: "Nod's Friend."

31. Stephanie Says So

After fleeing the bank in anger, Stephanie Knight-leigh had roamed the town for some time muttering to herself. When she finally arrived home, it was almost two in the morning, and her mother was waiting by the door.

"Where have you been, young lady?" Judith Stainsworth-Knightleigh demanded. "Your father and I have been worried sick. We need you at full strength if you're going to help us solve this hunt. Sleepyheads do us no good. Isn't that right, dear?"

The mayor grumbled from a nearby armchair, where he had fallen asleep in his gargantuan pajamas and fuzzy slippers.

"Mmm, quite right. Stephanie, what's the meaning of this late-night activity?"

Normally Stephanie would rue such upbraiding from her parents, but tonight she didn't care. Tonight she wanted answers.

"Does the name Agatha mean anything to either of you?" she asked.

"Agatha?" said Mayor Knightleigh. "No, no, I don't think so." But his voice wavered ever so slightly.

Judith's eyes narrowed at her daughter.

"What are you talking about, Stephanie?" she asked.

"I think you know, Mother," Stephanie replied. "Agatha *Nod* Knightleigh, first wife to Pierre Knightleigh. Just how big *was* our family fortune after Thaddeus died?"

"How did you—*where* did you—" sputtered the mayor.

"It doesn't matter. I want the truth."

"You want the truth?" said Judith in a dead voice. "Fine. The truth is this: There never was a Knightleigh fortune. Thaddeus drove the family finances into the ground, so when Pierre and Agatha fell in love, he was more than happy to marry them off, thinking she'd eventually inherit all of Nod's wealth."

"But that hateful old buzzard loathed us Knightleighs so much, he disowned his own daughter!" snorted the mayor.

"Yes, he thought he had cut us off for good," said Judith. "But then he disappeared and left no will. By default, Agatha ended up with her father's fortune after all. She died shortly after that, leaving Pierre a rich, rich man."

"But Nod *did* leave a will," said Stephanie.

"We never knew about it!" cried the mayor. "Of all the rotten luck! Why did this happen during *my* reign? And my plan was so brilliant—"

"What plan?" snapped Stephanie.

"Er, well, I thought that, well, if *I* were to find the golden limbs, then we'd finally own Nod's inheritance fair and square."

"*You* planted the fake limbs," said Stephanie. "Of course you did. Daddy, if you had just told me, I would have helped—I would have made sure it went off without a hitch! Now your townspeople are crazier than ever!"

"Don't talk to your father that way," said Judith. "What could *you* have done? Besides, no one else knows the history. *If* someone manages to find the limbs, they'll have no idea the true wealth they're entitled to."

"As a matter of fact, two other people know all about it," said Stephanie.

"*What?*" shouted her mother and father at once.

"Those twins were with me when I discovered everything. They'll keep quiet for now—it's not in their interest to blab until the hunt's over—but you can bet that their big mouths won't stop talking after that."

"Would—would anyone believe them?" asked the mayor. His eyes darted back and forth.

"Don't you see? It wouldn't matter," said Stephanie. "I've never seen the town like this. All it will take is the suggestion. We didn't have to look very hard to find Agatha's story. There are probably other records like this in Herringbottle's files that back it up, and our greedy townspeople won't stop until they find them."

"It—it can't be," said Judith. "There are no records."

"Are you absolutely sure, Mother? Are you willing to bet our whole fortune on it? Our credibility? You haven't been all that popular since the *Better Homes Than Yours* fiasco—what would you do if you were further disgraced?"

"Stephanie! That's enough!" But Judith's voice shook. She reached into the pocket of her robe and removed a monogrammed handkerchief to dab her eyes.

Stephanie hesitated. She had never seen her mother cry before.

"You can't let it happen, Stephanie!" wailed her father. "You can't let them take everything away! What will we do? What will we do?"

"I just wanted to be a good hostess. It's all I ever wanted. That and fabulous shoes," Judith blubbered.

Stephanie looked at her parents, awestruck. They had always been in control, and now, when things really mattered, they could barely form coherent sentences.

Stephanie stood as tall as she could and put her hands on her hips.

"Mother. Daddy. No one is going to break this family. Especially not two vagabonds who don't even *have* shoes. I have a plan."

Stephanie explained her scheme to her parents, who nodded weakly as their tears dried. Shortly afterward she left the house again, and neither the mayor nor Judith protested.

However, Stephanie had not noticed her little brother sitting at the top of the stairs. Miles sighed mournfully; never had the boy looked so disappointed.

32. Ye Olde Switcheroo

"We have to make it sound like one of the regular clues," said Edgar. He hovered over Ellen's shoulder as she tried to compose the false clue they would plant at the bridge. "But it's got to be easy enough to be figured out quickly. We need to get everyone in town over here and digging."

"And it will go much faster without you breathing down my neck," said Ellen.

Edgar glanced back at Pet, who still lay unconscious in its nest, breathing shallowly. The creature looked as flat as a deflated balloon.

When Ellen was finally satisfied with her handiwork, the twins had one more detail to attend to.

"We're about to invite hordes of prying eyes into our house," Edgar said. "The last thing they need to see is the one-eyed mystery wig."

"You're right," said Ellen. "But where can we hide Pet?"

Edgar looked out the window and felt a pang of guilt as his eyes fell on their old caretaker's dilapidated shack.

"We can hide Pet in Heimertz's shed," he said. "No one would look for gold in that rickety old thing."

Once Pet had been safely tucked into an open accordion case, the twins ran all the way to the Cairo Avenue bridge. When they looked up at the ceiling—as "perched above the floor" seemed to indicate—they saw only the rafters, supported by thick beams that spanned the bridge.

Edgar walked the length of the bridge. "'By one, then two, then three, then four.' Here! The fourth beam! Could it be that simple?"

In a hole in the top of the fourth timber, the twins found a small, folded piece of parchment.

"This is it!" said Edgar. "Let's see what it says. . . ."

"Later, Edgar," said Ellen. "We still have a lot to do before dawn."

The twins replaced the parchment with their homemade clue, then dashed back toward their house. But instead of turning up the nameless lane, they crossed onto the property of the Knightlorian Hotel next door.

The lobby was quiet, with one security guard fast asleep behind the front desk. From past ventures into the Knightlorian, the twins knew that the room assignments were kept in a file cabinet. Unfortunately the guard's chair was smack-dab in front of it.

Ellen crept up beside the guard. His feet were kicked up on the desk, and his hands were folded across his chest. He snored pleasantly.

"Here, hold his feet," said Ellen.

"Are you crazy? He'll wake up."

"No, he won't. There are light sleepers, heavy sleepers . . ." Ellen pointed to a small puddle on the floor. "And then there are drool sleepers. Move him."

Edgar frowned, then gently lifted the guard's legs off the desk, struggling under their weight.

The guard groaned and recrossed his arms.

"Don't drop them!" whispered Ellen.

"You . . . try . . . lifting . . . tree trunks . . ." grunted Edgar. He tugged on the legs, and the chair rolled aside.

"Okay, let's see," said Ellen as she perused the files in the cabinet. "Looks like the whole cast and film crew are staying here."

"Just find what we're looking for!" Sweat started dripping from Edgar's brow. "I can't hold these much longer. . . ."

"Here, I've got it. Room 1013. Let's go."

Just then, Edgar's fingers slipped, and he dropped the security guard's legs. They hit the floor with a giant *thud*. The guard sprang to his feet.

"Wha—who's there?" he cried, looking around. But he was all alone, and as he settled back into his chair to resume his nap, he failed to notice the elevator's pointer going higher and higher, until it stopped on the tenth floor.

When the twins reached room 1013, the Presidential Suite registered to Blake Glide, Edgar pulled a tourist map of Nod's Limbs from his satchel. He spread it out on the floor.

WELCOME FRIEND TO NOD'S LIMBS STAY AWHILE was handwritten across one side of the bridges' roofs, and COME BACK SOON FRIEND AND TAKE CARE, was written on the other. The twins had drawn a circle and stars around the Cairo Avenue bridge, along with the words, "Be sure to visit this beautiful, historic site!"

"Too obvious?" asked Ellen.

"You can't be too careful with this mental lightweight," Edgar replied.

The twins slid the map under the door and returned to the elevators.

"With any luck, hordes of hunters will soon be banging on our door, demanding to dig up our foundations!" said Edgar.

33. Bamboozled

The sun was rising over the eastern hills as the twins ran back to their house to work on the clue they'd found at the bridge. But first, they ducked into Heimertz's shed to check on Pet.

The creature slumbered in the accordion-case nest and did not stir when Ellen stroked its hair.

"Time to save Pet," said Edgar. He unfolded the clue and read it aloud:

> *You think you're clever, you've followed the clues,*
> *Well, won't you be shocked when you hear the news,*
> *This whole hunt was fake! I hope you don't mind,*
> *But there never were any gold limbs to find!*
> *Ha ha!*

The twins were silent for several minutes.

"It—it can't be," said Ellen. "The whole thing was one big wild goose chase? Why would Nod go through all the trouble?"

"We know that he hated pretty much everybody in town," said Edgar thoughtfully. "One last joke from the grave?"

"I can't believe we've been pranked by a guy

who's been dead for 200 years!" said Ellen. "It's . . .
it's . . ."

"Impressive," finished Edgar. "We should try
something like that when we get old and crusty."

"Edgar, this isn't funny! The will's a sham! Without the limbs, how will we get our house back?"

Ellen patted Pet on top of its closed eyeball.

"I'm sorry, Pet," she whispered. "We did our
best. But your old pal pulled our legs from beyond
the grave."

"Ellen, there's still our fake clue at the bridge,"
said Edgar. "No one else knows the hunt's not real.
People will still flock here with their pails and picks
and shovels. We may not be able to save our house,
but at least we can still save Pet."

34. The Hobo and the Pirate

Later that morning, a peculiar figure could be seen
walking toward the Cairo Avenue bridge. He wore
baggy pants and a polka-dot shirt, and had long,
straggly brown hair. His Coke-bottle glasses made
his eyeballs look three times larger than normal, and
he walked with a cane.

People passing in their cars paid him little notice, until Miles Knightleigh ran by on his fake peg leg.

Something about the man's walk made Miles pause—Miles lifted up his eye patch for a better look, and saw a large, bronze ring on the man's hand. It had a bulging bicep embossed on it—the ring every die-hard fan would recognize as the prize for winning a Best Muscles award from the AAA—the Action Actors' Academy.

"Mr. Glide! Mr. Glide!" shouted Miles. "Where are you going? Can I come, too? Why are you dressed like that?"

"Quiet!" said Blake Glide. He glanced around for eavesdroppers. "No one's supposed to know it's me."

"Got it," squealed Miles, snapping his eye patch back into place. "Are we undercover? In-cog-neato? Awesome! I can be undercover too, see? *Arrr!*"

"Yes, yes, that's swell. Now if you want to come, hush up!" said Blake Glide.

"Okeydokey," Miles whispered. And the two continued up Cairo Avenue, the short, clownish man and the tiny pirate.

"This is just like when you went undercover as a garden gnome in *The Slurminator*! You sure showed those giant pus-sucking larva!"

"Why, thank you. It's always important to really try to embody a character, to get inside its head and say, 'Hey, what would a real garden gnome do in this situation.' Uh, but that's beside the point," said Blake Glide. "We've got to stay focused here."

"Focused. Right. Totally focused," said Miles. But focusing was hard since he practically had to run to keep up with the movie star and the peg leg kept slipping out of place.

As they approached the river, they passed Stephanie's best friend Cassidy Kingfisher, who was on her way to Knightleigh Manor. Cassidy looked skeptically at the oddly dressed man, but recognized the young pirate.

"Miles, what are you doing?" she asked, pulling him aside. "And who is that creep?"

"Mr. Glide and I are undercover," Miles

whispered. "I don't know where we're going, but we're getting there fast!"

"Undercover?" said Cassidy. "Why would you be—Ooh, are you following a clue? I'll bet you are, aren't you?"

"Mr. Glide would probably want me to say no," Miles said.

"Aha! Thanks, Miles!" Cassidy shouted, running off.

"No problem!" Miles called back.

Blake Glide had kept walking, hoping Miles would be sidetracked enough to forget about him. What he did not know was that, next to the mayor himself, Cassidy Kingfisher had the biggest mouth in all of Nod's Limbs. As she ran toward Knightleigh Manor to tell Stephanie the big news, she let slip to everyone she met along the way that Blake Glide had figured out the fifth clue and was, even now, striding up Cairo Avenue toward the river.

35. Shall We Gather at the River?

By the time Blake Glide and Miles reached the Cairo Avenue bridge, a crowd had collected behind them. The action star sighed heavily as he realized his attempt to go incognito had failed.

"B. G.! You figured out the clue, and you didn't tell me?" Otto Ottoman pushed his way through the throngs. "I'm hurt, Blake, baby. It hurts me, right here it hurts me." The director tapped his chest.

"You were going to fire me!" cried Blake Glide.

"That doesn't mean I don't love and respect you," Otto Ottoman replied.

The rest of the Nod's Limbsians were getting impatient.

"Where's the clue? What's the answer?" came shouts from the crowd.

Just then, the mayoral limo pulled up and the mayor, Judith, Stephanie, and Cassidy jumped out of the car.

"What is the meaning of this?" asked the mayor, bulldozing through his citizens. "I didn't call a town meeting or a press conference, and I know it's not Love Our Bridges Day, because that's next month!"

"The clue! The clue!" shouted the Nod's Limbsians. "Blake Glide has the answer to the clue!"

"Does he now," said the mayor. He glanced at Stephanie, who nodded ever so slightly, then turned back to Blake Glide. "Well, then, congratulations,

Mr. Glide! Your intellect truly matches your acting ability!"

"For once, the mayor speaks the truth," said Edgar. He and Ellen had been hiding beneath the bridge, waiting patiently for Blake Glide to pick up on their blatant hint.

"So, *Nod's friend* is the bridge that bears the words," the mayor continued, putting his arm around the movie star. "You are a credit to the acting community! Well, sir, go get that clue!"

"Uh, right," said Blake Glide, and, with all of Nod's Limbs watching breathlessly, he stepped onto the bridge.

Blake Glide poked around for a while, but he didn't really know where to look and didn't find anything resembling a clue. Ellen was about to march up to him and point out the hiding spot when Stephanie called out, "Um, maybe it's in one of those beams up there, Mr. Glide."

"The beams! Yes!" cried the townspeople. "But which one?"

"I would, uh, try the fourth one," said Stephanie.

"At least she's serving some kind of purpose," said Ellen, but Edgar looked troubled.

"She seems to have all the answers, Sister," he

said. "I'm glad we got to the clue when we did. A few hours more and we might have been too late."

"Yeah, too late to learn there wasn't any gold to begin with," Ellen muttered.

"How do we get up there?" asked Blake Glide.

"Never fear, we've got ladders!" came a voice from the crowd. Fire Chief Gully Lugwood stepped forward with the rest of the firefighters, a couple of whom carried retractable ladders. "We always travel with them, in case of an EKR—Emergency Kitten Rescue!"

The firefighters set up their ladders on the fourth beam.

"Can I climb up to get it?" asked little Timmy Poshi.

"I think you're too small, son," his father replied, "but as neighborhood watch commander, I'd be happy to—"

"Very noble, sir," said Police Chief Gomez, shoving his way onto the bridge, "but this is a matter for the authorities, and I should probably—"

"Now wait just a doggone second, Gomez," said Gully Lugwood. "These are my ladders, I know how to climb them best—"

"But I was the one who figured out the clue!"

Blake Glide protested. "I should be the one to get it. Plus I do all my own stunts!"

"Now, now," said the mayor. "In the case of a stalemate, the mayor always casts the deciding vote, and I've decided that *I* should be the one to get that clue—"

The townspeople surged onto the bridge as everyone sought a chance to retrieve the clue.

"Oh, for cripes," said Ellen. "This is ridiculous. Will one of them just get it already? Pet is *dying*."

"Not even you and I argue this much," said Edgar, shaking his head.

36. My Kingdom for a Clue

Finally Stephanie scooted past all the bickerers and climbed the ladder herself. Everyone fell silent, except for Blake Glide, who whined, "Not fair. *I'm* the famous movie star."

Stephanie reached the beam and promptly found the small hole where the twins had hidden their clue. She pulled out the piece of paper.

"Got it!" she shouted triumphantly, descending the ladder.

Once on the ground, Stephanie unfolded the paper. "Shall I read it out loud?" she asked.

"Yes! Yes!" cried the Nod's Limbsians impatiently.

"Okay, here we go." Stephanie looked down smugly at the clue, but her face paled as she read it over. "Wait," she said, almost to herself, "this isn't right. . . ."

"Oh, give it here, then," said Blake Glide, snatching the clue from her hand. "Let a professional actor give it a proper reading."

He cleared his throat and in a booming voice, read out:

Cluck like a chicken and squeak like a mouse,
It's time to head to the towering house!
Slip down the stairs to the cavern below,
Follow the arrows, they show where to go.

"Towering house?" said Mr. Poshi. "The tall gray eyesore by the hotel?"

"It must be!" called Suzette Croquet.

"At last!" said Blake Glide. " A clue I can understand."

The mob needed no further prompting, and made for the twins' house, looking more like a buffalo stampede than an orderly Nod's Limbsian parade.

Edgar and Ellen, however, stayed put.

"Did you see Stephanie?" said Edgar.

"I know," said Ellen. "She looked shocked."

"It's almost like she expected the clue to be something else," said Edgar. "Plus, she knew right where to look. . . ."

With the crowd now cleared, the twins saw Stephanie, at the other end of the bridge, her brow still furrowed in puzzlement. She looked up to see the twins staring back at her. Then she snarled, and her fingers curled into trembling fists.

"You planted that clue!" Stephanie and Ellen yelled at the same time. They strode toward each other, fury in their eyes.

"The hunt hasn't ended at all!" shouted Ellen. "Of course! You just wanted everyone to *think* it was a hoax, so no one would challenge your family's ill-gotten wealth!"

"You put that clue in the rafter," Stephanie seethed. "Why? Why send everyone to your own house? What are you up to?"

"Where's the real clue, Stephanie? Where is it?" Ellen dove at her nemesis. "You rotten, vomitous, scum-skinned toad!"

"I found it first, you greasy pipe-cleaner!" Stephanie jumped out of the way just in time.

Ellen came at her again, and this time, Stephanie wasn't so lucky. Ellen bowled her over, and the two girls rolled across the bridge, pulling hair and scratching skin.

"Ouch!"

"Quit it!"

"Get off me!"

"Had enough, cream puff?"

Edgar, who until this point had cheered on his sister but had wisely chosen to sit out the fight, noticed something slip out of Stephanie's pocket. It was a small metal tube. Edgar snatched it up, and out fell a scroll of paper tied with a golden thread.

"Sister! Sister! I've got it! I've got the clue— *Oomph!*" Stephanie had managed to untangle herself from Ellen and grabbed Edgar's knees, toppling him.

"Give me that!" she screamed, lunging at the clue, but Edgar tossed it over to Ellen.

"Sister, catch!"

"Ha! Monkey-in-the-Middle! You're familiar with monkeys, right, Steph? Your family's full of them."

"I'm . . . never . . . the monkey!" Stephanie shrieked, so forcefully it startled even Ellen. Stepha-

nie charged toward her, but Ellen just threw the clue back to Edgar.

Maybe it was because she was so excited, or maybe she didn't remember where she was standing, or maybe she just didn't know her own strength, but Ellen threw the piece of paper just a little too hard, and it sailed right past Edgar and out a bridge window.

"Now look what you've done!" cried Stephanie. She and the twins raced to the window, but, despite the Running River's snail-paced current, they could see no hint of the clue. It had sunk, or dissolved, or simply been swept away.

"I can't believe it," Stephanie murmured and buried her head in her hands.

"What do you care?" asked Edgar. "You wanted the hunt to end anyway. Now it has. For good."

Stephanie looked up, clenching her teeth. "I wanted to *win*."

37. Setting Sail

"Uh, Stephie? Stephie, can I talk to you?" Miles had appeared at the end of the bridge.

"What do you want, Miles?" barked Stephanie.

"Um, this landed on the riverbank." Miles held up the piece of paper. The gold thread had fallen off, but the twins and Stephanie knew instantly what it was.

They ran at the boy, but Stephanie got there first. She grabbed the paper with one hand and unsheathed Miles's wooden pirate sword with the other.

"Stay back," she yelled, swinging the sword to keep the twins at bay as she scanned the clue. "Back! I'm warning you—no! No! It can't be!" Stephanie clutched the note and fled, pirate sword in hand.

"Miles!" Edgar said. "I thought we were allies! How could you give the clue to *her*?"

"She's my sister," said Miles. "She'd beat me up if I gave it to you."

"But—but—" Ellen stammered. Her lip was dripping blood and her footie pajamas were even dirtier than usual from her tussle with Stephanie. "Oh, never mind. Come on, Edgar, we've got to follow her."

"I remember what it says," said Miles quietly.

"What?" Both the twins stopped abruptly.

Miles recited:

From where I stand, I look down on you all
Your egos so big, your virtues so small.

'Mad' some have called me, and in the same manner,
I call you all fools from my roost in my manor.

"*My manor?*" cried Edgar. "He means his—I mean, *our*—house!"

"Oh no," said Ellen. "We sent everyone there— The whole town is already at our house! We've got to get back there!"

"But where to look?" said Edgar. "The clue didn't mention any specifics. It could be anywhere in the whole house."

"What's a . . . a *Bordox*?" asked Miles.

"Not now, Miles," said Ellen.

"I think it's important. See, I had to give Stephie the riddle, because she's my sister. But she's being really mean—er, meaner than usual—so I didn't give her *everything*."

"What do you mean?" asked Edgar.

Miles held up a torn fragment of paper.

"I tore off the last lines. They tell you where to look."

"Great Bluebeard's ghost!" exclaimed Edgar, plucking the paper from Miles' hands. "It's not *Bordox*—"

Edgar showed Ellen the scrap:

From Burgundy to Bordeaux,
The world's in your grip,
Now sail on past Port
For one final trip.

"I've seen some of these words before," said Edgar.

"Of course you have," said Ellen. "Bordeaux, Burgundy—They're places. France, I think."

"Not just that. I've seen them in . . . in our house somewhere."

The twins thought for a minute, until both Edgar and Ellen shouted, "The wine casks!"

> *Oh, what fools we've been! What folly*
> *Not to guess Nod's grand finale!*
> *The seat of all his melancholy,*
> *His home, of course. That fox!*
> *Hurry! Hurry! The crusading*
> *Hunters are by now invading,*
> *Hear the rasping, jarring, grating,*
> *Shovels mine the rocks.*

38. An Ancient Double-Cross

In some homes of a certain age, enormous oak barrels in the cellar are remnants of a long-ago era of extravagance. In those days the filthy-rich kept an abundance of wines and brandies and other luxuries to shower on guests (and themselves) as a sign of status. But for most of the twins' lives, the sturdy casks in their subbasement provided not status, but crevices to hide in and perches to pounce from.

Recently they had discovered that one of the casks did not hold liquid at all, but a secret set of stairs. This barrel was actually a hidden door to a passageway that led to the cavern beneath their house—and to the balm spring.

Edgar called after Ellen as the twins ran back to their house.

"But, Sister," he panted, "we inspected all the casks after we found the secret passage. Every one was empty."

"Well, we must have missed something," Ellen replied, "because the wine casks *have* to be the answer to the riddle—holy smokes, look at this!"

The gold-hungry mob had wrenched the twins' front door from its hinges. When the twins reached the subbasement, they could hear the frantic *schik-schick-shick* of hundreds of shovels at work in the cavern below.

"Move your keister, Matterhorn!" called a muffled voice. "That's my dirt mound!"

"Get your pickaxe out of my pile, Poshi!"

"I never did like your butterberry muffins, Buffy!"

Edgar and Ellen's plan had worked perfectly: The treasure hunters had followed the twin's arrows (some cut from plywood, some hammered out of tin, some chalked onto the floor), which had led them down the stairs to the balm pit.

"The greedy devils," said Ellen. "They'll reach the spring in no time. Pet will be saved!"

"Hurry, let's check the casks for those limbs," said Edgar.

The wide, round faces of the casks rose twice as tall as the twins themselves. Each bore a sign identifying the wine within: BORDEAUX, BURGUNDY, PORT.

"Nod mentions all of them but this one," Ellen said, stopping before the rightmost cask, which read AMONTILLADO.

"That's it!" said Edgar. "You sailed *past* Port, Sister!"

Edgar threw open the door and entered the belly of the barrel.

Even in the dim lights of the subbasement, it was clear that the wine cask held only cold, dank air.

"Empty," said Edgar. "The hunt's a bust."

"Give me your flashlight," said Ellen.

"Sister, it's over," said Edgar.

"Give it to me!"

Edgar rooted the flashlight out of his satchel and handed it to his sister. Ellen shone the light over every inch of the interior, as if waving it like a magic wand might conjure up some golden limbs.

It did not. But just before turning off the light, she noticed something else hidden in the dust.

A mildewed envelope.

"No!" groaned Edgar. "No more riddles! We solved all six, Nod! We beat you, you old coot!"

Ellen picked it up gently as if the crisp, decayed paper might disintegrate altogether.

"Brother, I don't think this is a clue. Look."

The front of the envelope, in words so faded the twins could barely read them, was addressed TO MY OLD FRIEND AND COLLEAGUE, THE ESTIMABLE AUGUS-TUS NOD.

Ellen pulled out a handwritten letter. The beam of the flashlight revealed faint words:

Dearest Augustus,

Well, well, well. What have we here in this old barrel? I can't say I am surprised to find the so-called "stolen limbs" stowed away in <u>your</u> home. Unlike our fellow citizens, I have never believed the simple stories of their theft. Vindication! What were you planning for them, I wonder? No matter. They're mine, now. It seems Providence favors the "dull-witted laggard" you sacked from the Waxworks, eh, Augie? Take that to your grave!

Signed most sincerely,

Thaddeus

P.S. Vote Knightleigh!

"Swindled!" cried Ellen. "You can't even trust a *dead* Knightleigh."

Edgar threw the note on the ground and stamped on it. "Thaddeus, you loathsome pustule! You rotten sack of louse larva—"

Edgar's string of curses was cut short by a scream from the cavern below.

39. Bone-a-Petit

"I—I was just digging, and my shovel struck something." Betty LaFete had turned as gray as an overcast day. "And then I saw a foot! I thought—I thought it might be one of the limbs—but then I realized, it wasn't a *gold* foot at all—it was a *bone* foot!"

Diggers crowded around for a look. Sure enough, the bones of a foot protruded from the dirt, and a little farther up, they could see a few skeletal fingers.

Edgar and Ellen pushed through, hoping that someone had unearthed the spring. They spied the foot and sagged in disappointment.

"Rats," said Ellen. "It's only Nod."

The twins had already found these bones on an earlier adventure, when a dirt collapse had nearly killed them.

"Nod? Did you say *Nod*?" cried Betty LaFete. "Have I dug up our town founder? Am I cursed?"

"The clothes look old enough," said Ernest Hirschfeld, examining a nearly disintegrated velvet waistcoat. "Could it be that Augustus Nod buried himself with his treasure?"

"Who cares? I smell gold!" shouted Marvin Matterhorn, throwing his shovel back into the ground.

"Rest-thee-well, gentle sir," said Sir Malvolio, bowing respectfully to the skeleton. Then he jammed his spade into the earth with a gleeful snort.

The rest of the Nod's Limbsians followed suit, abandoning the remnants of the town founder without another moment's thought. They worked steadily, delving deeper and deeper into the dirt. As they toiled, their flashlights dimmed and darkened one by one—but even this couldn't slow them, and they made crude torches to light their way. In flickering firelight, they burrowed ever on.

"They're going to make it!" whispered Ellen at last. "Our plan worked!"

"It all comes down to good scheming," said Edgar.

Just then, Calvin Hucklebee's shovel broke through to an open space.

"I found it! I found it!" he shouted. His older brother nudged him in the ribs. "Oh, I mean, nope, didn't find anything."

But it was too late. The treasure hunters attacked the dirt wall with their shovels, digging until the chamber beyond revealed itself. Stale air drifted out, and the townspeople covered their noses. For all their ardor, nobody dared venture into the cave. They hesitated on the edge of the opening, no one daring enough to step inside.

No one, that is, except Edgar and Ellen.

The twins pushed to the front and peered into the darkness.

"This is it," whispered Ellen.

"*Our* treasure," breathed Edgar.

The twins were about to plunge in, when out of the blackness came a low but distinct *skitch . . . skitch...skitch.*

Something was in there.

Something *alive*.

40. Greatest Show Unearthed

Everyone heard it. No one moved.

Hundreds of pairs of eyes gazed at the black hole, and then they could just make out a stir in the shadows.

Skitch . . . skitch . . . skitch . . .

A bent form caught the glow of the torchlight.

Snarled heaps of dark, grimy hair covered the creature from top to bottom, seeming to bristle and
writhe. The onlookers stumbled backward over one
another, speechless with dread.

Skitch . . . skitch . . .

Slowly, the thing shambled closer.

A musty gust from the grotto rustled the beast's
tangled hair, exposing a wide, yellowish eye.

"Brother"—Ellen dug her nails into Edgar's
hand—"It's . . . it's . . . a giant *Pet*."

Blake Glide finally broke the silence.

"GAAAAA! A FLESH-EATING SLURM!"

The action star fled, knocking aside all in his
way.

When they saw their hero run, the entire lot of
treasure hunters dropped their buckets, shovels, and
torches and scrambled after him.

"Our greed has loosed a demon!" howled Buffy.

"Why couldn't I have been content with a life of
lawn care?" wailed Chief Strongbowe.

"I don't want to be a pirate anymore!" cried Calvin Hucklebee.

Only the twins remained, though they dared not
approach the creature. Then, two pale, spindly arms
reached out from beneath the veil of hair.

"Arms?" cried Edgar. "This is no Pet!"

The creature drew closer. The black pupil of its eye expanded and contracted like a beating heart.

Edgar ransacked the contents of his satchel for anything that might keep the beast at bay: his claw hammer, his wrench—*anything*. At the bottom he found an old bicycle pump and aggressively pumped the handle.

"Don't make me use this, fiend!" he growled.

Ellen struck an absurd kung-fu pose.

"I have a black belt in eye poking, Cyclops," she said as she snaked two fingers in the air and hissed.

The creature stepped through the threshold of its lair, stretched to an astounding height, and howled. The twins grimaced and covered their ears as the wail echoed through the cave. The thing lurched forward and snatched the twins up, pressing them against its coarse, rank hair. The twins squirmed and kicked, but could not break free.

"Put us down!" cried Ellen. "I'm warning you!"

"Don't underestimate us, you festering—*oof!*" The grip tightened and expelled the remaining air in Edgar's lungs.

With the twins helpless in its hold, the pillar of hair bellowed again; but the cry softened into a hyena-like cackle, and settled finally into deep, rich, *human* laughter.

"GLORY BE, I'M FREE!"

The hairy mound spun in a mad circle, laughing and hopping with Edgar and Ellen in tow. "Children! Sweet, sweet children! The most beautiful things I have ever seen!"

"Who are you calling *sweet*?" Edgar snapped.

"Beautiful?" Ellen snarled. "You dare!"

The shaggy figure dropped Edgar and Ellen to the ground and danced a rickety jig. In the light of the half dozen torches abandoned by the treasure hunters, the twins saw that the dreaded "slurm" was not a flesh-eating monster at all, but a man—an old but lively man in serious need of a bath and haircut.

"Who are you?" asked Ellen.

"Who am I? Who *am* I? Hmm." The old man stopped spinning. With long, ragged fingernails he pulled aside his filthy mane like curtains in a haunted mansion and revealed a second eye, bright and full of life.

"Last time someone addressed me—mind you, that was some time ago"—A magnificently crooked smile spread across his face—"I believe they called me . . . *Augustus*. Yes, that's it. Augustus."

"Augustus?" the twins repeated in unison.

"Augustus Nod. Pleasure to make your acquaintance."

41. Say Good Knightleigh

"Nod?" Edgar blinked.

"Nod's *Limbs* Nod?" Ellen tilted her head and squinted.

"Nod's *Lands* Nod," corrected Augustus. He coughed. "Some harebrained jesters renamed my municipality after the disappearance of my statue's limbs—"

"Forget about disappearing limbs!" shouted Ellen. "What about the reappearing *you*?"

"It's not possible," said Edgar. "You'd be more than 200 years old. . . . We—we found your skeleton!"

"Skeleton? Well, it's not mine, I can assure you," said Nod. "You need not believe it for it to be true. How I survived I will never reveal, but—"

"Balm!" exclaimed Edgar. "Can it be? Is it powerful enough to keep you alive all this time?"

"You know of my Life Balm?" asked Nod. "Alas,

it is as I feared. My imprisonment left too many details unguarded in my laboratory. It stands to reason such secrets could never lay undiscov—NO TORCHES!"

The old man sprang at Edgar, who had picked up a torch and approached the musty tomb.

"Don't worry. We know all about the balm's explosive properties. You mentioned it in that journal of yours—and I have firsthand experience to back it up." Edgar wedged the torch in a crevice, a safe distance from the threshold.

"My private works—*you* young ones have read them?"

"Yes," said Ellen. "It was about as exciting as reading the ingredients on a tube of toothpaste."

"*Toothpaste?* Now who would use a paste made from *teeth*?" asked Nod.

Ellen grabbed two metal buckets and rushed into the chamber. "As much fun as it is hanging around an unstable cave, chewing the fat with a 200-year-old relic, we're on a mission."

The twins ventured into Nod's prison. They saw little in the flickering light, but they could hear something ahead. . . .

Gurgle, gurgle. Blip, blip, bloop.

Something cool splashed Ellen's cheek. She wiped it away, but her skin continued to tingle. "Balm . . ."

Their eyes adjusted to the dim light, and they found themselves in a grotto about the size of a doctor's waiting room. The only furnishings were an itchy-looking mattress made of Nod's own hair and a few stones that had been crudely chiseled into the shapes of tops and building blocks. In the middle was a pool of gooey liquid that bubbled forth from the earth.

"We really did it, Ellen. We found the spring."

Nod shuffled in behind them.

"Astounding, is it not? For thousands of years, man has searched for a spring of eternal life. Deluded seekers had naught to guide them but myths, shadows of hope to the desperately mortal. But I found it."

"Could it actually bring you back from death?" asked Ellen. "Even if you got hit by a train or something?"

A familiar voice spoke from the grotto's entrance. "We could certainly test that theory, Ellen."

Stephanie Knightleigh stepped in from the tunnel.

"Good instincts, sweetheart," said Mayor Knightleigh, following her.

"I told you the twins were behind all this, Daddy."

Judith Stainsworth-Knightleigh appeared beside her husband, holding a torch. "And it is high time we put all this dirty business behind *us*."

The Knightleigh family stepped into the chamber. Gone was the brash smile worn by the jovial, crowd-pleasing mayor. Gone was the jolly man who had headed so many silly parades and ridiculous festivals. Instead Mayor Knightleigh's eyes had become piercing black bullets, and his lip curled more than Stephanie's hair.

"You are trespassing on my property," he said, picking up a pickaxe. "And in my town, trespassers are prosecuted to the fullest extent of the law."

42. Remains of the Dead

"I would recognize that triple chin anywhere!" said Augustus Nod. "You, sir, must be the slimy seed of none other than that gluttonous scoundrel, Thaddeus Knightleigh!"

"Hey!" yelled Stephanie "Whoever, or whatever, you are—You are in the presence of power!"

"I am in the presence of criminals!" Nod spat. "Thaddeus Knightleigh was a fiend so wretched that any descendent of his must be equally as crooked!"

"Spot on, old-timer," said Edgar.

"We can vouch for that," agreed Ellen.

"Now see here! No one speaks about my great-great-great-great-great-great-great-grandfather Thaddeus that way! Or about *me*!" roared Mayor Knightleigh. "I don't know who you are or what you are doing down here . . ."

Judith Stainsworth-Knightleigh stepped next to her husband. "But the laws of our town clearly forbid the habitation of transients within our borders. No soup kitchens, no shelters, no homeless. It's bad for tourism."

"You morons," said Edgar. "Do you have any

idea who this man is?" He pulled two handfuls of Nod's long, dirty hair away from the old man's face. "Doesn't he look a little familiar?"

Mayor Knightleigh grabbed the torch and held it closer to the man before him; the light bathed Nod's face and the mayor peered carefully at him. Suddenly he stumbled back.

"N-n-n-not possible!"

"Stand your ground, you—" began Judith, but she choked as recognition dawned on her too. "Oh my heavens!"

"A ghost!" shrieked the mayor.

Only Stephanie stood firm. "Daddy, he smells too gross to be a ghost." She examined the gnarled old man in front of her. "But you do look an awful lot like the statue of Augustus Nod."

"Indeed, for I am he!" Nod answered.

"But how—?" Stephanie began, then glanced at the twins. She shrugged. "You know, I should be shocked. Yet somehow, when it involves you two freaks, I find that few things genuinely surprise me anymore. Whoever you are, old man, I don't have time for this."

"But the limbs—we just wanted the limbs—the limbs were all," the mayor babbled.

"Look no farther. *Here* are Nod's limbs!" quacked Nod, kicking out his skinny arms and legs. The mayor shuddered.

"Why are *you* looking for them?" asked Edgar. "It was *your* ancestor who took the golden limbs."

"WHAT?" cried Stephanie.

"Yes, so he did," said Nod. "That blathering nincompoop Thaddeus intruded upon my house, looking for the rumored 'secret ingredient' that made Waxworks candles burn so bright. Before he could uncover such mysteries, he stumbled upon my golden limbs—the luck of an idiot! He stole them from me, as sure as crabapples are tart. But the simpering backstabber wasn't content with that, no! He returned later, still bent on finding my candle secrets. This time he managed to come upon me in my laboratory. Couldn't stop gloating about the limbs, could he? That is, until he caused the explosion that trapped me underground—" Nod stopped. "There's a skeleton down here, you say?"

"Right over there," said Ellen, pointing back to the pile of bones that stuck out of the ground.

"Woo hoo ha ha!" Nod laughed. "Who'd have guessed? All these long years I have cursed Thaddeus for his treachery, and it turns out he went and got himself buried under the rubble of the explosion *he* caused!"

"You mean," began Ellen, "you mean that skeleton is *Thaddeus Knightleigh?*"

"I'd bet my life on it," said Nod. "And I have a lot of life to bet!"

"That's a lie. Thaddeus is buried in his tomb," said Stephanie, kneeling beside the skeleton. But when she looked among the bones, she noticed a signet ring with a familiar crest.

"Daddy—Daddy, it's the Knightleigh crest!" she cried. "This *is* Thaddeus!"

43. Burying the Truth

"Nod . . . two hundred years old if he's a day . . . *the* Nod . . ." Mayor Knightleigh stammered while Judith Stainsworth-Knightleigh wrung her hands.

The twins slipped back into the grotto. Stephanie watched them fill buckets with balm as she mused to herself.

"If Nod's 'will' spelled disaster for us, what will his *existence* mean to the Knightleigh legacy?" She yanked the flickering torch from her mother's white knuckles and moved closer to Nod.

"Stephanie!" shouted Ellen. "Don't!"

"Keep that fire back!" Edgar yelled.

"Listen, mister, I don't care how you managed to stay alive all this time. I don't care why you're here and what you want. The little treasure hunt you left for us? It caused quite a stir."

"Young lady," Nod said calmly, "no matter your agenda, I can assure you, that torch will cause a great deal more than a stir."

"You think you can trick me, old fool?" said Stephanie. "If that skeleton is Thaddeus, I bet *you* murdered *him*! He learned about your twisted underground experiments and tried to stop you—"

"ENOUGH!" Nod thundered. "You insolent, iniquitous, treacherous frogspawn!"

"Frogspawn," said Ellen. *"Nice."*

"Your beastly ancestor brought fire to the balm spring and triggered a devastating explosion," Nod continued.

Stephanie smiled. "Is that so?"

"Oops," Edgar said.

"Too much information, Nod," added Ellen.

"But that's what happened, dear twins," Nod replied. "He was waving that blasted torch of his as he boasted and accidentally lit a glob of balm. . . ."

Stephanie pointed her torch at the balm-filled buckets. "Balm? This stuff?"

"Stephanie, do you really think you'd fare better than old Thaddeus?" asked Ellen.

"Of course. You're talking to the under-twelve champion of the Spring Is Sprung Sprint. Daddy, Mother—why don't the two of you go back upstairs?"

The mayor and his wife did not need a second prompting. They clattered back up the tunnel into the cavern.

Ellen stepped in front of Nod. "Listen, Stephanie. You think I'm despicable and I think you're . . . well, frogspawn pretty much covers it. But what you're about to do . . . It would be *murder*."

"Technically? Not." Stephanie pointed the torch at Nod. "The way I figure, whatever kept him alive all these years will do the same for you. You'll be kicking and screaming down here for centuries." She paused. "I can live with that."

Stephanie Knightleigh dropped the torch into a bucket.

The last thing the twins saw were Stephanie's auburn curls dashing into the blackness of the tunnel, followed by a blinding flash.

And then everything went black.

44. A Touching Farewell

KABOOM!

The explosion came from underneath the mansion. On the twins' front lawn, the crowd of treasure hunters screamed as the earth quaked beneath them, knocking many to the ground. The house before them swayed ominously and creaked like a redwood in a windstorm.

"Revenge of the slurms!" cried Blake Glide, his award-winning biceps wrapped tightly about Janitor Clunch. "Nowhere to run! Nowhere to hide! The slurm army shall wreak their vengeance!"

"The whole town will be sucked into the abyss for its greed!" cried Mrs. Elines. "Forgive my selfishness! I only wanted to use the gold to build some luxurious whirlpool suites in my humble motel!"

"The shame!" wailed Buffy. "How could I abandon the noble taste of scones for the bitter, cold tang of gold?"

"Wait, where is our mayor?" called Principal Mulberry. "Did he get out of the building? *Where is our mayor?*"

"*There!*"

The crowd erupted in jubilation as Mayor Knightleigh and Judith barreled out the front door of the creaking mansion followed closely by Stephanie. Clouds of dust and ash belched from the door and windows, and chunks of slate and rock broke off the swaying house, peppering the Knightleighs as they escaped.

"Sweet cream of corn!" exclaimed Principal Mulberry. "Our mayoral family is alive!"

"Any slurm bites?" asked Blake Glide. "Check for slurm bites, people! That's how they multiply!"

Mayor Knightleigh glanced at his daughter, cleared his throat, and drew his gut up into his chest. Back in the sunlight, he quickly forgot his fears.

"My fellow Nod's Limbsians, it seems our treasure hunt has come to an unfortunate end. Sadly, there was an unexpected cave-in below. The limbs—and the horrible creature guarding them—have been claimed by the earth. The golden treasure shall be recovered nevermore."

45. Return to Sender

The blast had hurled Edgar and Ellen against the opposite wall, and they strained to get their bearings in the blackness. Rock and rubble poured into the tunnel, sealing the grotto's exit.

"My head," groaned Edgar.

"My ears," whined Ellen.

"I think I hurt my bottom," said a meek voice between them.

"Miles?" cried the twins.

Miles Knightleigh clicked on a penlight and held it under his pudgy, eye-patched face. "Arrr."

"Where did you come from?" Ellen demanded.

"I was here the whole time."

"You were?" Edgar asked. "We didn't see you."

"Oh, I'm used to that," said Miles. "I snuck down here to help you."

"Stop your chitchat and get to digging!" barked Nod.

Just then a chunk of cave fell loose from the ceiling between Miles and the twins, followed by a flood of pebbles and dust. They could hear a creak in a nearby wall, followed by a crack and the sound of cascading rock.

"This cavern couldn't withstand a second explosion," Nod said. "It is about to come down upon us."

"Your sister condemned us to die down here, Miles!" yelled Edgar.

"So that little purple troll is your sister, eh, boy?" cried Nod. "At least this cavern will claim another Knightleigh before I perish."

"As Knightleighs go," said Ellen, "this one's all right."

"Aw, thanks, El-*aaaigh*!" Miles caught a gob of earth in his mouth. Another chunk of the ceiling gave way, and Ellen hugged the remaining bucket of balm as boulders fell over the mouth of the spring.

KRAAAAK-OOOOOM!

"Dig for it!" cried Edgar. "Get to the surface!"

"It's no use," said Nod. "We would need the strength of a hundred men, and we are but four—three too young and one too old. This shall be our tomb."

A rupture raced up the nearest wall and across the ceiling. The twins and Miles screamed in terror as a river of dirt and silt poured down from above. But even in the dim penlight, Edgar noticed something emerging from the crack in the wall. It looked at first like thick, fleshy worms. And then he realized what they were.

"I know those fingers!"

A slab of earth toppled out of the wall like a ten-ton domino.

THOOOOM!

A behemoth of a man wriggled out and dropped before them. He had hands the size of boulders, legs the girth of two oak trees, and a gleaming smile that seemed wider than his head.

The twins raced into his waiting embrace and hugged their rescuer with all their might.

"HEIMERTZ!"

KRAAAAK-KOOOOOM!

With a single sweep of his mighty arm, Heimertz gathered the twins, Nod, and Miles, and shoved them into the channel he had come through. The passage felt narrow as a gopher hole, but it was enough room for the five of them to crawl up to the floor of the grand cavern.

But the cavern too had felt the effects of the blast. Sheets of earth dropped from the walls and stone rained from above.

"We'll never make it!" Nod cried.

As they dashed for the stairs, the cavern collapsed, burying the lab, the tunnels, and the balm spring beneath tons of earth.

46. Everyone Still Loves a Parade

". . . And so let this tragic day linger long in our memories," said Mayor Knightleigh, "well into next week, after which we can all forget about such glum and grisly matters and kick off our seventh annual March of the Mini-Mayors parade!"

Sniffles and sobs faded momentarily at the mention of the word "parade." The mayor noticed the change in mood.

"Yes, my flock! Parades . . . plural! Lots of them!" Mayor Knightleigh's voice boomed. "Parades! Festivals! We shall never again dwell upon the gold bug that threatened to burrow into our very hearts! Golden limbs? Bah!"

Calvin Hucklebee approached the mayor with his pirate hat in his hands. "Where is Miles, Mr. Mayor?" he asked. "I sort of owe him an apology."

"Miles . . ." Stephanie said, snapping her head toward the house. "He wasn't—he couldn't have been in the . . . No, he *must* be around here somewhere."

"Yes," Judith whispered to her daughter. "Where is that boy? I put him in your charge."

Stephanie rounded on her mother. "You expect

me to crush our mortal enemies *and* watch my little brother?"

Glass crashed behind her, and the citizens turned to the tall, narrow house that now leaned cruelly in the darkening sky.

"A structure like that can't take the strain of all that swaying—" Eugenia Smithy began.

"GREAT GALLOPING GALILEO!" cried Marvin Matterhorn. "It's coming down!"

Indeed the walls began to buckle, casting down a hailstorm of broken stones.

Stephanie had waited forever for this moment. She had endured a lifetime of rivalry and one-upmanship, an eternity of aggravating pranks and calculated sabotage conceived in the dark halls of this house. And while everyone around her gasped in alarm at the sickening sounds of the structure twisting in its socket, Stephanie smiled.

At least, she smiled until five dusty figures ran out the front door.

A pirate, a giant, a walking mound of hair, and lastly—side by side as Stephanie always saw them in her nightmares—two pale twins in striped footie pajamas.

47. Up and Crumbling

Miles, Nod, Heimertz, Edgar, and Ellen raced out of the house just as the cupola slid off the top, like the upper tiers of a melting wedding cake. The cupola spun as it fell. The wrought iron spikes of the roof, which had pointed skyward for more than two hundred years, now sliced toward earth at astonishing speed.

"She's breaking apart!" shouted Nod. "Stand clear!"

The spikes speared the dirt right behind them as they dove for cover behind Heimertz's shed. The cupola shattered, showering them with splintered wood and glass.

The house swayed one last time, then split open, like a pirate galleon dashed on a rocky coastline. With a tumultuous shouting sound like the voice of a thousand waters, the mighty walls rushed asunder. The house launched its guts—furniture, globes, organ pipes, suits of armor—onto the lawn.

Then the dank earth closed sullenly and silently over the foundation of the towering house at the end of the nameless lane.

The twins peered out from behind the shed with

mouths agape and lips quavering—even Nod seemed stunned. It was Miles who finally spoke up.

"Wow," he said softly.

The twins turned to Heimertz. He was panting heavily, and though his smile never drooped, his head and arms looked painfully bruised and bloodied.

Ellen stared up at him. "How . . . ?"

Heimertz took Ellen's letter from his pocket and shook it gently. Edgar held out his palm as his favorite lock pick tumbled from the creased paper and into his grip. Then the caretaker's smile slid off his face, and he slumped to the ground with a groan.

"Heimertz!" cried the twins.

"Ronan!" shouted a woman behind them.

Madame Dahlia, mistress of the Heimertz Family Circus' Botanical Beastiary, emerged from the shed and propped the fallen man's head on her shoulder.

"Ronan, we escape from one jail together," she said softly. "Do not now escape somewhere else I cannot follow."

Heimertz opened his eyes and softly patted her cheek. A half-hearted grin wavered on his face.

"Thank the stars!" Madame Dahlia said as she dabbed at Heimertz's wounds. "I will nurse my darling back to health. He will live. I fear another may not, however. Our littlest friend . . . is having the death look." Madame Dahlia took out a bundle of rags from the folds of her skirt and handed it to Edgar. He unwrapped the bundle carefully; a tuft of hair lay within.

Pet was now entirely white, and it looked up mournfully at the twins with a gray eye, its pupil ringed in red. The twins gasped.

"Unless some miracle you have planned, this is your Pet's ending hour," whispered Madame Dahlia as Pet's eye closed.

48. Pet's Cemetery

"Pilosoculus!" Nod exclaimed before the twins could respond. "Why, you look terrible, old chap! Young lady, let's save the rascal, shall we?"

"Yes, definitely!" said Ellen, holding out the bucket of balm she had rescued from the cave-in. "You're not done yet, Pet!"

Edgar gingerly laid Pet in the bucket, and the creature sunk below the surface of the white balm.

"Is—is that what's supposed to happen?" asked Edgar.

"Watch closely, my boy," Nod replied.

The small group huddled around the bucket gazing into it as if it were a crystal ball. Even Miles dared not speak.

The townsfolk had watched the collapse from a safe distance, but now they drew nearer the destruction and the curious band of survivors in its midst.

Still, nothing stirred in the bucket. At last an orb the size of an orange floated to the surface of the goop: an eyeball.

Closed.

"No," whispered Ellen. "Pet!"

"But we made it in time!" said Edgar.

"Pilos," murmured Nod. "Would you please . . . quit . . . *teasing*!"

At this, Pet opened its eye wide. It leaped out of the goop and into Ellen's arms. Miraculously the color was already rapidly returning to its hair, and its eye gleamed yellow as ever.

"For Poe's sake, Pet, you're going to pay for that one!" said Edgar, but his smile stretched so impossibly high up his face it looked as if it might fly off his cheeks. The twins swung the creature around and around and tousled its hair until it was again back to its black, matted snarls.

Pet's eye—so cloudy and dull moments ago—now sparkled at the old horseplay, until it caught sight of Nod. Nod gazed back at it, tears in his eyes.

"Pilos—all these years I thought that surely you were dead, for your lifesource was bound with me. It was my fault, my petty feud with a petty man that put you in danger. I am sorry I abandoned you, old friend." Nod stopped, choking on the last few words.

Pet merely blinked and sprang into the old man's shaggy beard. Nod hugged the creature and tousled its tendrils.

"Good to see you again, you rotten old pile of whiskers," he said.

49. The Awakening

"Miles!" cried Stephanie. "You were in there? How? Are you okay?"

Miles didn't respond. He turned his back on his sister and plopped onto the ground, arms folded.

By now the townsfolk had finally drawn close enough to get a good look.

"Mama?" asked Penny Pickens. "Who's that big bundle of hair?"

The old man wheeled about and faced the crowd. He placed Pet on his shoulder and bellowed.

"Quit gawking like fish on a plate and say good day! These gape-jawed expressions are no way to greet your town founder!"

The crowd gasped.

"Founder? Nod? Ridiculous."

"That's impossible!"

"Hey, his limbs aren't gold!"

"Oh, I am he, all right. Augustus Nod! And these two heroic children have released me from two

189

centuries of internment within the presence of—well, some natural compounds that suspend death beyond all natural law! For two maddeningly solitary centuries I was held captive underground by the greedy design of Thaddeus Knightleigh!"

Lyman Herringbottle stepped out from the crowd, pushed his spectacles up the bridge of his narrow nose and studied the hairy man. "Most curious . . ."

Nod pointed a long, bony finger at the Knightleigh family. The mayor, Judith, and Stephanie had receded behind the townspeople and continued to slink slowly toward the limousine.

"Knightleigh cretins!" Nod bellowed. "Go no farther!"

The citizens of Nod's Limbs looked anxiously at the howling old man, then at their mayor and his family, and then back to their accuser.

"He's clearly mad . . . right?" stammered the mayor. "No one could believe such a claim . . . Could you?"

"Silence! Your townsfolk shall know of your treachery! And you shall pay a price for this wickedness." Nod seemed to tower over the crowd now. "The mayoral torch passed from generation to corrupt generation in your family is hereby extinguished!"

"YOU CAN'T DO THAT!" screamed Stephanie. "I'M THE NEXT MAYOR!"

"You wouldn't make a very good mayor, Stephie." Miles dropped his pirate hat and eye patch in the dirt. "You tried to explode this man. And Edgar and Ellen." He swallowed hard. "And me."

"Miles! I had no idea you were even there!"

Cries of astonishment rose from the crowd.

Meanwhile, Lyman Herringbottle removed his spectacles, wiped them clean, and put them back on. He squinted and tugged a wiry tuft of Nod's beard. "Similar jawline . . ."

"You don't deserve to be mayor, Stephie," said Miles. "Not ever." He looked up at his mother and father. "And you don't either, Dad."

The few citizens who stood near the Knightleighs now took a step back.

"Is't true, my mayor?" asked Sir Malvolio. "Didst thou try to . . . *harm* these poor children . . . and this o'er-bewhiskered gent?"

The buzz of the crowd grew louder, and the mayor stumbled toward them with his arms open.

"Friends . . . neighbors . . . Nod's Limbsians . . . ," he called. "I . . . I . . . of course I didn't try to harm these beautiful children!"

"Liar!" cried Ellen. "You set off the explosion that destroyed everything we own!"

"But we lived to tell your dirty tale," said Edgar.

"Why did you let Stephie try to kill us?" asked Miles.

Mayor Knightleigh whipped around and pointed his fat finger directly at Stephanie. "It was *her* idea!"

"DADDY!"

"She lit the fire that caused the explosion!" The mayor looked desperately to his wife. "Isn't that so, dear! Tell them! We wanted nothing to do with such madness!"

Judith looked at her daughter coldly. "I tried to raise her properly. Wrote, and then read her all the right books, sent her to all the appropriate seminars . . . but it seems—"

"JUST LIKE THE SCOUNDREL, THADDEUS KNIGHTLEIGH!" boomed Nod. "You would say anything to save yourselves! But this day you shall be undone by your own greed and deceit!"

"Fascinating!" Lyman Herringbottle, finished with his inspection of Nod, giggled and shook his head. He addressed the townspeople, who were frozen and fixed on the startling revelations about their mayor and his family. "Ladies and gentlemen of the town of Nod's Limbs, as strange as it may be, this man is indeed our town founder."

"I couldn't agree more," said Nod with a grunt.

"Look here above his left eyebrow—you've all seen it on the statue," said Lyman Herringbottle. "Here it is: the birthmark, shaped like a spider. Nigh-indisputable evidence!"

Not a murmur or cough could be heard from the transfixed crowd.

"I cannot explain how he has endured for two hundred years," continued Lyman Herringbottle. "I know little of the laws of nature. I do, however, know the laws of the land. And since this is indeed the man himself, I can only follow the basic dictates of my profession: Augustus Nod, in light of your unexpected reemergence, you are officially restored ownership of all your assets and estates."

"We know where his money went!" said Edgar. "It was wrongfully inherited by—"

"I know full well who inherited Nod's wealth," said Lyman Herringbottle, fixing the Knightleighs with a stern gaze. "I have been doing a little exploring among our records at Herringbottle, Pratt, and Filbert, and they have proven to be exactingly complete. I'm afraid the Knightleigh family will find itself parted from a significant sum of cash and land holdings by this time tomorrow."

"Did you hear that, villains?" Nod asked. "No? Well, let me state it plainly then: GET OFF MY LAND, KNIGHTLEIGH FLOTSAM!"

Nod's eyes bulged beneath his shaking mound of hair. Some in the crowd began to boo the mayoral family.

The mayor, his wife, and Stephanie ran to the limousine at full speed. Before she ducked inside, Stephanie turned and yelled.

"We'll be back on top again," she cried. "Just like that hairy fossil over there, a Knightleigh *never says die!*"

The limo peeled down the road toward Knightleigh Manor.

"Forgotten again." Miles sighed. "Good."

50. You Can't Go Home Again

Having spent days in a spiraling cyclone of greed and madness only to then be witnesses of wanton destruction, attempted murder, and mayoral disgrace, the good people of Nod's Limbs had little energy left to muse over the miraculous reappearance of a two-hundred-year-old man.

"I'm pooped," confessed Mrs. Elines as she walked away with her husband.

"Me, too, lovebird. I could use a good nap."

Blake Glide walked off toward the Knightlorian. "I sure would have preferred real gold over a really old guy," admitted the movie star. "I'll be completely broke after this flop of a movie comes out."

"I think this means we'll need to nominate some candidates to replace Knightleigh," said Becky Faff. "You know, Mr. Glide, I'm betting you'd make one heck of a mayor. . . ."

"You think so? Well, I did play a police commissioner in *Lethally Handsome II: When Looks Kill*. Yeah, I think politics come pretty naturally to me. . . ."

"Bah! Two hundred years and you people are still sheep," said Nod. "Who ever heard of an actor running for *office*?"

"Better go fire up old Annabelle, rookie," Chief Strongbowe said to Nathan Ruby. "Time to restore some much missed Lawn and Order to Nod's Limbs."

"Come, good knight." Sir Malvolio clapped a

hand on Sir Geoffrey's shoulder. "Our fair bridges need a fresh coat of Soothsayer Scarlet."

"That's the really bright red paint, right?"

Sir Malvolio rolled his eyes as the two men alighted their saddles and galloped east.

As Augustus Nod and Lyman Herringbottle discussed the legal ramifications of the town founder's return, the rest of the townspeople dispersed with surprisingly little fanfare, mumbling things such as: "Gold is where the heart is," "The only golden rule is kindness," and "Buck yourself up! Tonight is meatloaf night!"

Edgar and Ellen sat together on the lone step left intact at the base of their former home. They could see Miles kicking pebbles down the lane, and Dahlia tending Heimertz, but they didn't have the energy to console friends at the moment. Ellen traced her finger along the word "Schadenfreude," which was etched across broken stones in the rubble.

A healthy Pet bounced buoyantly amid the wreckage. Then it dove into the ruins and emerged with one of Edgar's slingshots between its shiny, black tendrils. It playfully wagged it at the twins, but neither cracked a smile.

"Thanks, Pet," muttered Edgar.

"Yeah, Pet." Ellen let out a huge sigh. "I mean I'm glad you're going to be all right and all. I really am. But . . . our house . . ."

"Where will we live now?"

The twins looked like wilted weeds.

"Why so glum, ragamuffins?" Nod asked lightly as he shuffled over to them.

"Everything we had . . ." Edgar gestured at the junk-covered lawn.

"Everything we own . . ." Ellen lifted the torn canvas of her favorite work of art: an oil painting of moldy cabbage and eggs.

"Own?" said Nod. "Why do you lament over matters of ownership? You are sitting on my property!"

The twins stood up. "Are you saying you want us to go?"

"Oh, sweet children," said Nod. "*Of course* I want you to go. I'm a hermit! Can't stand people. Not a one of them. Leopard can't change his spots, you know."

The twins stood in dumbfounded silence.

"Well, off with you, then," said Nod, and he turned to pick through the rubble.

"You evil, evil, dust mop of a man," murmured Ellen.

Pet leaped into the old man's arms. Nod chortled and grabbed the creature by the scruff. "Ho! No, my little beast, *you're* not going anywhere. We shall live as friends again!"

There was nothing for the twins to do but shuffle off, away from the only place they had ever called home. They glanced back once. Pet wiggled a tendril, but Nod did not notice. He was still chattering away, now admiring the Knightlorian, where purple banners on the rooftop waved in the late afternoon wind.

51. The Final Riddle

Edgar and Ellen wandered aimlessly down Ricketts Road.

"Where—where should we go, Sister? If the Gadget Graveyard were still around we could build a shelter there—"

"But it's not around, is it? And besides, this is all Nod's property now, and he seems about as interested in sharing it as Knightleigh was."

"How about the forest? We could, er, camp for a while. Or we could live in the sewers."

"Of all Fate's wicked twists!" shouted Ellen. "When we said we'd give up everything to save Pet, I didn't think we'd actually have to give up *everything*! If we had just found those limbs!"

"Sister," said Edgar, cracking his knuckles. "What *do* you suppose Thaddeus did with the golden limbs? I mean, they've got to be out there somewhere—if we could find them, we'd have enough money to do whatever we want! We could leave Nod's Limbs for good!"

"Edgar, for all we know he melted them down to make golden water bowls for his poodles. They could be *anywhere*. And I've had enough of riddles for a lifetime."

"You're right, you're right," said Edgar. The twins continued walking silently in no particular direction.

"Still, something else is bothering me," he said after a long while.

"What's that?"

"If Thaddeus has been buried in the caves for all these years, what's in his tomb?"

52. Out on the Limbs

For two centuries the ornate mausoleum of Thaddeus Knightleigh stood just inside the gates of the town cemetery, providing a substantial monument to Nod's Limbs' first mayor.

"There's no mayor in here," said Edgar, looking at the name carved above the door. "Just Nod's Limbs' dirtiest secret."

As homes for the dead are provided with only modest security measures in a town like Nod's Limbs, Edgar's trusty crowbar had little difficulty cracking open the front door. Beyond lay a dark and stifling chamber.

The twins crept into the crypt, where a large sarcophagus rested atop a marble slab. On the sides were etched several scenes of a barrel-chested man—presumably Thaddeus Knightleigh—building a brick wall, saving children from a burning building, and, in one bizarre instance, wearing armor and slaying a dragon.

"I'm going to take a wild guess and say he designed this himself," said Edgar. "Especially the part over here where angels are feeding him grapes."

Beneath the angels was an inscription:

REST THEE WELL, SWEET THADDEUS.

LONG MAY YOU MAYOR IN THE HEAVENS.

"Somehow," Ellen whispered, "I don't think the heavens are where old Thaddeus has been mayoring."

Edgar pushed the lid of the sarcophagus. It budged slightly.

"Help me with this!"

Ellen wedged the crowbar under the lid and heaved. With the twins' combined efforts, they were able to slide the heavy slab aside by about a foot.

The twins looked wide-eyed over the lip of the sarcophagus. In the beam of Edgar's flashlight, they saw not bones, but limbs.

Four limbs.

Golden limbs.

The sound of clapping made them turn. There, in the doorway, stood Augustus Nod. And though it was difficult to detect amid the man's bushy hair, the fuzzy form of Pet protruded from an area that was probably the man's shoulder.

"You found the limbs, pups," he said. "You solved the puzzle."

"They're ours to keep!" said Edgar. "The will said so—"

"But I'm not dead, am I?" said Nod. "A will's not much more than inky parchment as long as a man is breathing."

"How did you even know the limbs were here?" Ellen demanded.

"Thaddeus always did have a flair for the dramatic. I had a hunch. This was the most . . . *theatrical* place he could conceive of, at least until he figured out what to do with them. A pity! He never had the chance, did he?"

"You're going to send us packing then, I suppose," said Edgar.

"Children," Nod said sternly, "I have been in deep consultation with my private councilor." He jerked his thumb toward Pet. "I am reminded that I once despised this town because none was worthy to be my heir. None had the gumption, the intellect, the *independent spirit*. But you two have proved me wrong."

"What are you saying?" asked Edgar.

"I've decided I may be able to extend an offer. Strictly for services rendered, you understand. But I'm going to need some assistance making my new home livable."

"Your home?"

"Yes. The so-called Knightlorian Hotel is standing on my land, and, as such, is *mine*. They got the basics right—tall and skinny, good bones—but they've almost ruined it with purple flags and neat rows of petunias. Would you be available to help set things straight?"

"Would we?" asked Edgar.

"I *do* have some decorating experience," said Ellen.

And thus the three humans and a Pet stepped merrily from the dusty mausoleum, each twin dragging a golden arm and leg and singing:

> *The seconds cheer: hoo-ray hoo-ray!*
> *As blackest hours melt away,*
> *And second chances rule the day—*
> *Let's turn that Knightleigh eyesore gray!*
> *Our house may be naught but debris,*

But Pet is saved and Heimertz, free,
With Nod returned in jubilee—
How strange—we've found a family.
Away the future winds and wends,
And only time may tell the end.

But when they reached the Knightlorian, they did not notice a limousine idling at the nearby cemetery gate. The back window rolled down and Stephanie Knightleigh peered out, her cheeks as red as her curls.

"So you figured out the final riddle first, did you? Well, that's okay," she murmured to herself. She looked down in her lap at a crusty bucket filled with white goop. "Because a Knightleigh never says die."

. . . It Ends

With an eye for the macabre and a near-unlimited budget, Edgar and Ellen began remodeling the former Knightlorian Hotel into a suitable new home. Edgar cleverly mixed hundreds of gallons of paint he had purchased from the Gallant Painstmen into a new, tar-like hue he dubbed Black Plague, and set Miles Knightleigh—a regular visitor now—upon the task of painting every wall inside the building.

"All by myself?" Miles had asked.

"Of course not!" Edgar replied. "You're a full-fledged captain of the high seas now, Scurvybeard. Recruit a pirate crew and put them to work!"

"Aye, aye, Edgar!"

Ellen and Dahlia set about rehabilitating the plants they had recovered from the destroyed greenhouse, including Ellen's dear, snapping Morella. Though many plants had been reduced to tatters, the effects of a collapsing house proved to be no match for Edgar's experimental "growth serums."

They picked among the rubble of the old house to salvage what they could. A particularly surprising find was the old telescope from their former attic-above-the-attic, which had miraculously survived the fall.

As they worked amid the debris, they took solace at a welcome sight: occasional visits from townsfolk, who heaved busted muffin-mixers or mangled mannequins or rusty rotary engines into the ruins. The town junkyard—Edgar and Ellen's hallowed Gadget Graveyard—seemed to be making a comeback.

Heimertz relocated his rickety shed to the foot of the Knightlorian. Now sporting a wonderfully menacing scar on his cheek, he resumed his aimless caretaking of the grounds with Madame Dahlia by his side.

In a matter of weeks, the determined twins, Miles, Pet, Heimertz, Dahlia, and the increasingly mischievous Augustus Nod managed to convert the hotel into (the twins had to admit) an even better version of the original tower mansion.

Instead of a dumbwaiter, Pet now coasted about the house at its leisure in an exceptionally fast elevator. Rather than spy at the town through slats of the attic-above-the-attic, the twins now found the views from each floor's balconies to be uniquely inspiring to their prank planning. And the saunas, hot tubs, and whirlpools throughout the interior made excellent homes for all of Ellen's and Dahlia's plants (Morella and the burly Gustav guarded the front gates with snapping jaws and flailing fronds).

One cool, fall night the twins sat atop the penthouse balcony, forced yet *again* to listen to Nod's ridiculously childish laughter as he heaved water balloons at Nod's Limbsians walking below.

"Weeee! Ha, ha!" Nod leaped up and down like a chimpanzee. After another successful water bombing campaign, he picked up Pet and tossed it playfully. "Did you see that, Pilos? A perfect strike!" The old man shouted to the street below. "You're a little wet behind the ears, Matterhorn! Hoo, hoo!"

Edgar tossed a grape into Ellen's open mouth.

"The possibilities are limitless now, Sister," said Edgar. "What shall we do first?"

"I seem to recall an old blueprint of yours, Brother . . . something about a windmill and giant pile of manure?" said Ellen. "Operation: Blowstink?"

"Yes," said Edgar. "Let's start small for now."

THE END

(SNIFF SNIFF)

BOOK I
Edgar & Ellen: Rare Beasts
Edgar and Ellen dream BIG when it comes to pranks. After they learn that exotic animals are worth tons of money, the twins devise a get-rich-quick scheme that sends Nod's Limbs into a frenzy!

BOOK 2
Edgar & Ellen: Tourist Trap
Mayor Knightleigh wants to turn little Nod's Limbs into a premiere vacation destination. But Edgar and Ellen have a plan to give the too-sweet townspeople all the attention they deserve!

BOOK 3
Edgar & Ellen: Under Town
Someone is causing a lot of trouble in town, but it isn't Edgar and Ellen! To catch this new mischievous miscreant, the twins must scour the sewers and uncover someone's dirty secret.

ischief begins...

Add to the adventure at
www.edgarandellen.com!

Enjoy Edgar & Ellen?
Add to the adventure at
www.edgarandellen.com!

Enter the Wonderfully Wicked World of Edgar & Ellen! Become a reporter for the *Nod's Limbs Gazette* and use your byline to share the horrible truth! Write your own mischievous tales starring Edgar & Ellen! Watch the cartoon or play the diabolically great games!

Experience
www.edgarandellen.com

Charles Ogden *is an avid camper and fisherman. He collects insects and has traveled in pursuit of various specimens to the North Pole, the South Pole, and Poland. Mr. Ogden and his insect collection make their home in a cool, dry, preservation-friendly environment, far removed from prying eyes.*

Rick Carton *has been drawing longer than he's been walking. In his Chicago studio he has a cherished collection of every pencil ever worn down to a nub during his lengthy artistic career. He has never formally studied art; instead, the art community has diligently studied him. They are yet to release their findings.*